# A MAN'S HEAD

One of the most significant figures in twentieth-century European literature, GEORGES JOSEPH CHRISTIAN SIMENON was born on February 13, 1903, in Liège, Belgium. He began work as a reporter for a local newspaper at the age of sixteen, and at nineteen moved to Paris to embark on a career as a novelist. According to Simenon, the character Jules Maigret came to him one afternoon in a café in the small Dutch port of Delfzijl as he wrestled with writing a different sort of detective story. By noon the following day, he claimed, he had completed the first chapter of *Pietr-le-Letton* (*The Strange Case of Peter the Lett*). The pipe-smoking Commissaire Maigret would go on to feature in seventy-five novels and twenty-eight stories, with estimated international sales to date of 850 million copies. His books have been translated into more than fifty languages.

The dark realism of Simenon's fiction has lent itself naturally to film adaptation with more than five hundred hours of television drama and sixty motion pictures produced throughout the world. A dazzling array of directors have tackled Simenon on screen, including Jean Renoir, Marcel Carné, Claude Chabrol, and Bertrand Tavernier. Maigret has been portrayed on film by Jean Gabin, Charles Laughton, and Pierre Renoir, and on television by Bruno Cremer, Rupert Davies, and, most recently, Michael Gambon.

Simenon died in 1989 in Lausanne, Switzerland, where he had lived for the latter part of his life.

For Nobel Laureate André Gide, Simenon was "perhaps the greatest novelist" of twentieth-century France. His ardent admirers outside of France include T. S. Eliot, Henry Miller, and Gabriel García Márquez.

# GEORGES SIMENON

## A MAN*S HEAD

TRANSLATED BY
GEOFFREY SAINSBURY

PENGUIN BOOKS

**PENGUIN BOOKS**

Published by Penguin Group

Penguin Group (USA) Inc., 375 Hudson Street, New York, New York 10014, U.S.A.
Penguin Group (Canada), 90 Eglinton Avenue East, Suite 700, Toronto, Ontario,
Canada M4P 2Y3 (a division of Pearson Penguin Canada Inc.)
Penguin Books Ltd, 80 Strand, London WC2R 0RL, England
Penguin Ireland, 25 St Stephen's Green, Dublin 2, Ireland
(a division of Penguin Books Ltd)
Penguin Group (Australia), 250 Camberwell Road, Camberwell,
Victoria 3124, Australia (a division of Pearson Australia Group Pty Ltd)
Penguin Books India Pvt Ltd, 11 Community Centre,
Panchsheel Park, New Delhi – 110 017, India
Penguin Group (NZ), cnr Airborne and Rosedale Roads, Albany,
Auckland 1310, New Zealand (a division of Pearson New Zealand Ltd)
Penguin Books (South Africa) (Pty) Ltd, 24 Sturdee Avenue,
Rosebank, Johannesburg 2196, South Africa

Penguin Books Ltd, Registered Offices:
80 Strand, London WC2R 0RL, England

First published as *La Tête d'un homme* 1931
This translation first published as *A Battle of Nerves* in
*The Patience of Maigret* by Routledge 1939
Published with *At the 'Gai-Moulin'* in Penguin Books 1950
Reissued, with minor revisions and a new Introduction in
Penguin Classics (UK) 2003
First published in the United States of America by Penguin Books 2006

1  3  5  7  9  10  3  6  4  2

Copyright © Georges Simenon Ltd, 1931
Translation copyright © by Georges Simenon Ltd, 1939
All rights reserved

Inside front cover author photo: © Georges Simenon Family Rights Ltd.

CIP data available
ISBN 0 14 30.3728 5

Printed in the United States of America

# CONTENTS

# CELL NO. 11

Somewhere in the Santé prison a clock struck two. The condemned man was sitting on his bed. Two large knotty hands gripped his knees.

For a minute, perhaps, he sat there quite still, tense, listening. Then with a sigh he stretched his limbs and stood up in the cell, huge, awkward, head too large, arms too long, chest hollow. His face expressed nothing, except a dull, blank stupidity, or perhaps inhuman callousness. Nevertheless, before reaching the door he shook his fist at one of the walls.

On the other side of the wall was a cell just like this, one of a row of cells in that department of the Santé known as the Grande Surveillance.

In this cell, as in four of the others, a condemned man was waiting. Waiting either for reprieve or for that solemn group who would come one night and wake him without so much as a word.

And for the last five days, every hour and every minute, this prisoner had groaned. Sometimes it was a dull monotonous whine, sometimes cries, tears, or shouts of fury. No. 11 had never seen him, nor did he know anything about him. All he could guess from his voice was that he was still quite young.

Just now the groans were tired, almost mechanical in their persistence. And a spark of hatred flashed into No. 11's eyes as he clenched that knotty-jointed fist.

From all around, from the passages and yards of that fortress that is the Santé, from the streets that skirted it, from the more distant quarters of Paris, there came no sound.

Nothing but the groaning of No. 10.

No. 11 tugged at one of his fingers spasmodically, shivered, shivered again, then reached for the handle of the door.

The cell was lit, according to the regulations of the Grande Surveillance. Normally, a warder should have been in the corridor looking hour by hour into the five cells of the condemned men. A spasm of anxiety shook No. 11 as he tried the handle. It was a fateful moment.

The door opened. The warder's chair was there, empty.

The man started walking quickly, giddily, bending low. His face was dead-white. Only the eyelids of his greenish eyes were reddened.

Three times he turned about, because he had lost his way and come up against locked doors. At the end of a passage he heard voices. A group of warders was talking and smoking.

At last he came out into a courtyard, the darkness of which was pierced here and there by a circle of light from one of the lamps. A hundred yards away, a man on sentry duty was walking up and down by a gate. In another direction a window was lit up and a man could be seen smoking a pipe, bent over a desk littered with papers.

No. 11 would have liked to consult the note he had found three days before, tucked in among his food, but he had swallowed it, as the writer had told him. An hour ago he had known it by heart, but now there were passages that were slipping from his memory.

> On October 15 at two in the morning you will find the door of your cell unlocked and the warder busy elsewhere. If you follow these instructions . . .

He ran a burning hand across his brow, shot a terrified glance from one lamp to the other, and nearly cried out when he heard steps. But they were on the other side of the prison wall. Free people talking to one another, while their footsteps rang out on the pavement.

"When I think of their having the cheek to charge fifty francs for a stall . . ."

It was a woman's voice.

"Oh, you know, they've got a lot of expenses," answered a man.

And the prisoner felt along the wall, stopped as he kicked a stone, and listened, so white, so unnatural with his absurdly long arms groping in the empty air, that in any other place you would have taken him for a drunken man.

They were hardly fifty paces from the invisible prisoner, a little group gathered in a recess by a door leading to some offices.

Inspector Maigret leaned against the dark brick wall. His hands stuffed in his overcoat pockets, he stood so stonily on his strong legs, and kept so still, that he seemed a lifeless mass. But at regular intervals came the wheezing of his pipe, and somehow you could guess the anxiety that he could not keep out of his eyes.

Ten times at least he had to nudge the examining magistrate, Monsieur Coméliau, to stop him fidgeting. The latter had arrived at one o'clock from some reception or other. He was in evening dress, his thin mustache carefully brushed up, his complexion redder than usual.

Beside these two was a third, Monsieur Grassier, the governor of the Santé. With a sulky expression on his face, his coat collar turned up, he pretended to take no interest in what was going on.

It was more than chilly, and the man on sentry duty stamped to warm his feet. At each breath a fine cloud was blown into the air.

They could not see No. 11, who avoided the circles of light. But, in spite of his care to make no noise, they could hear him coming and going, and could more or less make out what he was doing.

After ten minutes, the examining magistrate leaned over to Maigret and opened his mouth to speak. But the inspector gripped his shoulder with such force that he held his tongue, sighed, and mechanically took out a cigarette, which was promptly whisked out of his hand.

All three had understood. No. 11 had lost his bearings, and at any minute might be discovered by someone doing the rounds.

And they could do nothing about it. They couldn't very well take him by the hand and lead him to the knotted rope that hung down the wall, and beneath which was the bundle of clothes.

Sometimes a car passed along the street. Sometimes voices came over, echoing strangely in the prison yard.

The three men could only exchange glances. Those of the governor were snarling, sarcastic, savage. As for Coméliau, his nervousness was increasing every minute. Maigret was the only one to keep his composure and his confidence, but even so it was only by an effort of will. In daylight you would have noticed that his forehead was glistening with sweat.

When the half hour struck, the man was still wandering about. And then suddenly they were conscious of his feverish haste as he stumbled on the bundle of clothes and felt for the rope.

The sentry's steps still tapped out the passage of time. The magistrate could not help risking a whisper:

"You're quite sure . . ."

But Maigret shut him up with a look. There was the faintest sound as the rope stretched, and they could just make out a pale splodge against the wall—the face of No. 11 as he hauled himself up hand over hand.

What a time he took! Ten times, twenty times as long as they would have thought possible. And when he got to the top, it looked as though he'd chuck his hand in after all, for he did not move.

They could see him clearly now, in silhouette, lying flat on the coping.

What was the matter? Why didn't he get down the other side? Were there people about? A couple of lovers perhaps, hugging each other under the wall?

Coméliau was almost beside himself with impatience, while the governor said in a low voice:

"I suppose you don't need me any longer."

But at last the rope was hauled up and lowered the other side. The man disappeared. Coméliau could contain himself no longer.

"If I had not such confidence in you, inspector, I should never have got mixed up in such a business as this, I assure you. Don't forget, I still think Heurtin guilty . . . And now, suppose he slips through your fingers?"

"Shall I see you tomorrow?" was all Maigret answered.

"I shall be in my office by ten."

They shook hands in silence, the governor grudgingly. And he muttered something as he slouched off.

Maigret stopped a few moments by the wall. It was only when he heard somebody running for all he was worth that he walked to the gate. He nodded to the man on duty, gave a look into the empty street, and turned the corner of the Rue Jacques-Dollent.

"Gone?" he asked, speaking to a figure flattened against the wall.

"Toward the Boulevard Arago. Dufour and Janvier are on his heels."

"You can go to bed."

And Maigret absentmindedly shook the detective's hand and walked off ponderously, head lowered, lighting his pipe.

It was four o'clock before he pushed open the door of his office on the Quai des Orfèvres. With a sigh he took off his overcoat, then gulped down half a glass of lukewarm beer that was standing among the papers on his desk, and sank back into his chair.

In front of him was a file bulging with documents. On it, one of the scribes of the Police Judiciaire had written in a beautiful hand:

*Affaire Heurtin.*

————

He had to wait three hours. The unshaded electric bulb floated in a cloud of tobacco smoke that drifted this way and that with the slightest movement of the air. From time to time Maigret got up to poke the fire in the stove; then he would go back to his seat, discarding something on the way: his jacket, his collar, and finally his waistcoat.

The telephone was at his hand, and at six he picked up the receiver to make sure they had not forgotten to put his line through to the local exchange.

The yellow file was open. Police reports, newspaper cuttings, reports of the trial, and photographs had gradually spread over his desk. Maigret surveyed them from a distance. Now and again he would pick up a document, not so much to read it as to help him focus his ideas.

The case was summed up by a headline running across two columns of a newspaper:

*Joseph Heurtin, murderer of Mme Henderson and her maid, condemned to death this morning.*

And Maigret smoked incessantly, anxiously watching the telephone that was so obstinately mute. At ten past six it rang, but it was only a wrong number.

Leaning back in his chair, the inspector could read passages in the various documents before him. In any case he knew them by heart:

*Joseph Jean-Marie Heurtin, born at Melun, 27, rides a tricycle-van, delivering flowers for M. Gérardier, florist, Rue de Sèvres . . .*

There was his photograph, taken a year before at the fair at Neuilly. A tall lad with a pale face, triangular head, and abnormally long arms, dressed in clothes that betrayed a cheap swagger.

*Savage crime at Saint-Cloud. Rich American woman stabbed to death. Maid killed too.*

That was in July.

Maigret brushed aside the horrible photographs that had been taken on the spot: the two bodies viewed from every angle, blood everywhere, faces convulsed, nightgowns in disorder, torn, and bloodstained.

*Inspector Maigret of the Police Judiciaire has now cleared up the Saint-Cloud mystery. The murderer is in custody.*

He rummaged among the papers spread out in front of him and unearthed the newspaper cutting dated only ten days before:

*Joseph Heurtin, murderer of Mme Henderson and her maid, condemned to death this morning.*

In the yard below a police van was disgorging its harvest of the night, mostly women. Steps could be heard from time to time in the corridors, and the mist over the Seine began to lift.

The telephone rang.

"Hallo! Dufour?"

"Yes, chief. Dufour speaking."

"Well?"

"Nothing . . . at least . . . If you like, I'll stay here too . . . But for the moment Janvier's quite enough."

"Where are you?"

"At the Citanguette."

"At the what?"

"The Citanguette—a café near Issy-les-Moulineaux. I'll jump into a taxi and come and tell you all about it."

Maigret paced up and down, sending the office messengers to get some coffee and croissants from the café around the corner.

He was just starting to eat when Dufour entered, a meticulous, dapper little man, with his gray suit and high, very starched collar, and that air of mystery that was peculiar to him.

"First of all, what's this Citanguette?" growled Maigret. "Sit down."

"A café for bargees on the left bank of the Seine, between Grenelle and Issy-les-Moulineaux . . ."

"Did he go straight there?"

"Heavens, no. And it's a miracle he didn't shake us off. Janvier and me."

"Have you had any breakfast?"

"Yes, at the Citanguette."

"All right, then tell me all about it."

"You saw him get away, didn't you? Well, he started to run as though he was scared stiff of being caught again. He didn't feel safe till he got to the Lion de Belfort, which he stood and gaped at."

"Did he know he was being followed?"

"Certainly not. He never turned around once."

"Then?"

"Only a blind man could have gone the way he did, or someone who didn't know one end of Paris from the other.

He suddenly darted into the street that runs across the cemetery—I've forgotten its name. Not a soul about. Pretty grim. Obviously he didn't realize where he was till he saw the tombstones behind the railings. Then he started running again . . ."

"Go on." Maigret, munching a croissant, seemed already reassured.

"We got into Montparnasse. The big cafés were shut, of course, but one or two of the smaller ones were open. I remember he stopped in front of one. You could hear jazz being played inside. A flower girl came up to him, with her basket of flowers, and he moved on."

"In which direction?"

"One might really say in no direction at all. First he walked down the Boulevard Raspail, then turned back by a side street and stumbled on the Gare Montparnasse."

"What did he look like?"

"Like nothing at all. Just the same as when he was charged, or at the trial. Absolutely pale . . . and that vague, frightened look . . . I really can't describe it . . . Then half an hour later we were over on the other side of the river by the Palais Royal . . ."

"And nobody had spoken to him?"

"Nobody."

"And he couldn't have posted a note?"

"I could swear he didn't. Janvier followed along one pavement, I on the other. We never lost sight of him for a moment . . . He stopped once by a stall where they were selling hot sausages and fried potatoes. He seemed to hesitate. But a policeman was strolling in his direction, and off he went again."

"Did he seem to be trying to find some address?"

"Not a bit. He looked much more like a drunkard drifting about wherever his legs happened to take him. We got back to the Seine by the Place de la Concorde, and then he took it into his head to follow the river. Two or three times he sat down . . ."

"What on?"

"Once on the stone parapet. Another time on a seat. And that time, though I couldn't swear to it, he seemed to be crying. At any rate he had his head in his hands."

"There was no one else on the seat?"

"No one. Then on we went again. Just think of it—all the way to Moulineaux! Now and again he stopped to look at the water. A few tugs were passing up and down. Then the streets began to fill with workmen. And he just walked and walked like a man who hasn't the slightest idea of getting anywhere."

"Nothing else?"

"Nothing. But wait a moment—by the Pont Mirabeau he put his hand casually in his pocket and fished something out."

"The ten-franc notes."

"That's what we thought. Then he looked about him. Obviously looking for a café. But on the right bank of the river there was nothing open. So he crossed over. And in a little bar for chauffeurs he had a cup of coffee and a glass of rum."

"The Citanguette?"

"Not yet. Not by a long way. My legs were aching, and so were Janvier's. And no chance of *our* getting a drink to warm us up! He started off again, first this way, then that. Janvier wrote down all the streets and can tell you exactly. Then once more we were back by the river, near a big factory. Not a soul about . . .

"There were two scrap heaps, and between them some stunted trees and grass—quite countrified. A crane on the quay, and some barges lying alongside, perhaps as many as twenty . . .

"As for the Citanguette, it's a place you'd hardly expect to find there. A little bar where they serve food too. On the right there's a shed with an automatic piano, and a notice up: *Dancing every Saturday and Sunday*.

"The fellow had some more coffee and another tot of rum. Then they brought him some sausages, after making him wait a long time . . . He spoke to the man there, and a quarter of an hour later they both went upstairs . . .

"When the proprietor came down again, I went in and asked him straight out if he let rooms. He answered:

"'Why? Is there something wrong about him?'

"A man who's obviously had to deal with the police already. There was no sense in beating about the bush. Much better get him scared. So I told him point-blank that if he breathed a word to his customer, I'd have his place shut up.

"He'd no idea who he was sheltering. I'm quite sure of that. He caters mostly for the bargees, and at twelve o'clock the workmen from the factory come in for a drink . . .

"It seems that when Heurtin was taken upstairs he threw himself on the bed without even stopping to take his boots off. When the landlord objected, he took them off and chucked them on the floor. Then he went straight off to sleep."

"Is Janvier there now?" asked Maigret.

"Yes, he's staying. You can ring him up. The Citanguette has a telephone on account of the skippers, who often have to get in touch with their owners."

Maigret lifted the receiver, and a few moments later Janvier was at the other end of the line.

"Hallo! What's he doing?"

"Sleeping."

"Nothing suspicious?"

"Nothing . . . Quiet as a church here. From the bottom of the stairs I can hear him snoring."

Maigret hung up, and stared at Dufour, scrutinizing his slender person from head to foot.

"You won't let him get away?" he asked.

Dufour opened his mouth to protest, but the inspector laid a hand on his shoulder and went on still more gravely:

"Listen, old chap. I know you'll do all you can. But my position's at stake. Other things too. And I can't watch him myself, as the fellow knows me."

"I swear, inspector . . ."

"Don't swear. And now get along with you."

And Maigret turned abruptly to his desk, gathered up the straggling documents, and shoved the file into a drawer.

"And mind, if you need more men don't hesitate to ask for them."

Joseph Heurtin's photograph was still lying on the desk, and Maigret looked once again at the bony skull, the ears sticking out, the long, colorless lips.

Three mental specialists had examined the man. Two had declared:

*Of limited intelligence. Fully responsible for his actions.*

Only the third, called by the defense, had cautiously put forward:

*Some congenital deficiency. Responsibility subnormal.*

And Maigret, who had arrested Joseph Heurtin, had declared to the Public Commissioner, to the Public Prosecutor, and to the examining magistrate:

*Either he's mad or he's innocent.*

And he had set out to prove it.

He could hear Dufour's retreating steps as he trotted along the corridor.

## 2

# THE SLEEPING MAN

It was eleven o'clock when Maigret arrived at Auteuil. He had had a short interview with Monsieur Coméliau, trying in vain to reassure him.

It was a wretched day, the gray clouds only just above the roofs. It was dirty underfoot. Blocks of luxury flats looked down on him as he walked along the quay, while on the other side the scene was typical of Paris suburbs—factories, waste spaces, wharves with stacks of goods of every description.

Between these contrasting banks flowed the Seine, a leaden gray, its surface ruffled by passing tugs.

Even from that distance it was easy to spot the Citanguette, for it stood all by itself in the middle of a stretch of land littered with gear of all sorts: piles of bricks, rolls of roofing felt, scrapped cars, and even railway lines.

It was a two-story building, painted an ugly red, with three tables on the terrace. Some dock hands came out. They must have been unloading cement, for they were white from head to foot. As they left they shook hands with a man wearing a blue apron, presumably the landlord; then they strolled down toward one of the lighters moored alongside.

Maigret's features were drawn, his eye dull, but that was not due to a sleepless night. He would often let himself go like this. Each time, after pursuing his quarry furiously, his spirit would sag when at last it was within easy reach.

A sort of staleness that he could not shake off.

He picked out a hotel looking straight across at the Citanguette, and went in.

"I want a room facing the river."

"By the month?"

He shrugged his shoulders. He was not in the mood for arguing.

"For just as long as I like. Police Judiciaire!"

"We've nothing free."

"All right. Pass me the register."

"As a matter of fact . . . wait a moment. I must just find out whether No. 18 . . ."

"Fool," muttered Maigret between his teeth.

Naturally, they gave him the room. It was a high-class hotel. The porter asked him:

"Is there any luggage to fetch?"

"Nothing. Just bring me some field glasses."

"But . . . I don't know if . . ."

"Go on. Find me some field glasses, I don't care where."

He took off his overcoat with a sigh, opened the window and filled his pipe. In less than five minutes he was brought some mother-of-pearl field glasses.

"The manageress can lend you these. But she says will you . . ."

"Thanks. Clear out."

————

He already knew the front of the Citanguette by heart, down to the smallest detail.

One window was open upstairs. Through it he could see a rumpled bed, a huge eiderdown slipping down one side, some carpet slippers on a sheepskin mat. The landlord's room.

To one side was another window, this one shut. Then a third that was open and at which a stout woman in a camisole was doing her hair. The mistress, or perhaps the maid.

Below, the man in the blue apron was wiping the tables. At one of them Dufour was sitting with a glass of red wine before him.

The two men were evidently talking.

Farther off, down on the stone quay, a fair young man in a mackintosh and a gray cap was apparently watching the dockers unload the cargo of cement.

It was Janvier, one of the youngest members of the staff of the P.J.

In Maigret's room there was a telephone by the bedside. He lifted the receiver.

"Hallo! Is that hotel reception?"

"Can I do anything for you?"

"Yes. Get me through to that place opposite, on the other side of the river. The Citanguette."

"Very good," answered a prim voice.

It took a long time. But at last Maigret saw the landlord drop his duster and open a door. Then the telephone rang in Maigret's room.

"You're through."

"Hallo! The Citanguette? Will you please ask your customer to speak to me? Yes. You can't make a mistake as there's only one."

And looking out of the window, he could see the bewildered man go up to Dufour, who at once went into the telephone booth.

"Is that you?"

"Yes, chief."

"I'm over on the other side, in the hotel you can see from where you are. What's our man doing?"

"Sleeping."

"Have you seen him?"

"A little while ago I listened at the door. I could hear him snoring, so I opened the door a little and peeped in. He was lying all crumpled up, still in his clothes."

"You're sure the landlord hasn't given him the tip?"

"He's much too frightened of the police. He's already been in trouble, and they threatened to cancel his license. So he's on his best behavior now."

"How many exits are there?"

"Two. The main entrance, and a back door into the yard behind. Janvier's covering that one."

"No one's been upstairs?"

"No one. And no one can go up without my seeing

them, for the stairs are in the bar itself, behind the counter."

"Right! Have your dinner over there. I'll ring up again later. Try and look like somebody in the shipping business."

Maigret rang off, and dragged an armchair over to the open window. Feeling it cold there, he put on his coat again.

The girl below in reception rang up to know if he had finished his call.

"Yes. I've finished. Send me up some beer. And some tobacco."

"We haven't got any tobacco."

"Well, you can send for some."

At three in the afternoon he was still in the same place, his glasses on his knees and an empty beer glass by his side. In spite of the open window, the room reeked of tobacco smoke.

Thrown on the floor beside him were the morning papers with the official announcement:

*A condemned man escapes from the Santé.*

And from time to time Maigret shrugged his shoulders, crossed and uncrossed his legs.

At half past three, Dufour rang up from the Citanguette.

"Any news?" asked Maigret.

"No. He's still asleep."

"What is it, then?"

"The Quai des Orfèvres got on to me to ask where you

were. It seems the examining magistrate wants to speak to you at once."

This time Maigret did not shrug his shoulders, but dropped a good round oath. Then he rang off and put through an urgent call to M. Coméliau. He knew very well what the latter had to say.

"Is that you, inspector? At last! Nobody could tell me where you were. But at the Quai des Orfèvres they told me you had posted your men at the Citanguette, so I told them to find out from there."

"What is it?"

"First of all, have you any news?"

"Nothing at all. The man's asleep."

"You're quite sure? He's not got away?"

"With a little exaggeration I might say that I can actually see him sleeping at this moment."

"You know, I'm beginning to regret having . . ."

"Having taken my advice? But since the Minister of Justice himself agreed . . ."

"Wait a moment . . . The morning papers published your communiqué . . ."

"Yes. I've seen them."

"But have you seen the evening papers? No? Well, just get hold of the *Sifflet*. Of course I know it's a scurrilous rag. But all the same . . . Wait a moment. Don't ring off . . . Hallo! Are you there? Here it is: an article in the *Sifflet* under the heading *Reasons of State*. Are you listening, Maigret? I'll read it out:

*A semi-official announcement was made in this morning's papers to the effect that Joseph Heurtin, condemned to death by the Seine Assizes and awaiting execution in the Santé in the Quartier de la Grande Surveillance, had escaped under inexplicable circumstances.*

*We are in a position to add that these circumstances are not inexplicable to everybody.*

*As a matter of fact, Joseph Heurtin did not escape. He was made to escape. And this on the eve of his execution.*

*We are not yet in a position to give the details of the odious comedy that was played last night in the Santé, but we are able to state that it was the police officials themselves, in concert with the judicial authorities, who presided over this pseudo-escape.*

*Is Joseph Heurtin aware of the fact?*

*If not, we can find no words strong enough to qualify this operation, almost unique in the annals of criminal justice.*

Maigret listened to the end without turning a hair. At the other end of the line the examining magistrate's voice quavered.

"What do you say to that?"

"It only shows I'm right. The *Sifflet* people did not find that out all by themselves. And it wasn't one of the men who were in the secret who told them. It can only have been . . ."

"Who?"

"I'll tell you this evening. Things are going splendidly, Monsieur Coméliau."

"You think so? And suppose all the other papers reprint this stuff?"

"That'll make a scandal."

"You see . . ."

"Is a man's head worth a scandal?"

Five minutes later he was telephoning the Préfecture.

"Is that Lucas? Look here, old man. Run round to the office of the *Sifflet* in the Rue Montmartre. Get the editor by himself. Put the screws on. A little intimidation. We've got to know who gave him that information about the escape from the Santé. I'd bet my last franc he got a note somehow this morning. Get hold of it, and bring it here to me. Understand?"

"Have you finished?" asked the girl below.

"No, mademoiselle. Put me through to the Citanguette."

And a minute or two later Dufour was saying:

"Still asleep. I was up there just now for a quarter of an hour, listening at the door. And in his sleep I heard him mutter: '*Maman.*'"

————

Though his glasses showed him nothing through the closed window on the first floor of the Citanguette, Maigret could visualize the sleeper almost as clearly as if he had been there.

Yet he had made his acquaintance only in July, that day when, less than forty-eight hours after the Saint-Cloud murders, he had laid a hand on the young man's shoulder, saying quietly:

"Come along now! Don't let's have any nonsense."

It was in the Rue Monsieur-le-Prince in the modest hotel where Joseph Heurtin occupied a room on the sixth floor.

The landlady had said of him:

"A well-behaved, quiet young man. Hardworking too. He may have looked a little strange at times, but . . ."

"Did he ever have visitors?"

"Never. And except just lately, he never came in after midnight."

"And lately?"

"Two or three times he came in later. Once—that was Wednesday—he knocked us up just before four o'clock."

That Wednesday night was when the murders had been committed. The pathologists had said that the two women had died about two o'clock.

But without that, there was abundant evidence of Heurtin's guilt. And it was Maigret himself, more than anybody, who had collected it.

The house was on the road to Saint-Germain, about half a mile from the Pavillon Bleu, which Heurtin had entered at midnight, drinking four shots one after the other. When he paid, he dropped a single third-class ticket from Paris to Saint-Cloud.

Mrs. Henderson had been alone since the death of her husband, an American diplomat whose connections included some of the great financial families of the States.

Since his death, the ground floor of the house had not been used, the old lady living upstairs.

She had only one servant, who was really more of a lady-companion. This was Élise Chatrier, a French girl of good education, who had spent her childhood in England.

Twice a week a gardener came out from Saint-Cloud to look after the garden.

There were few visitors. Occasionally, at long intervals, a nephew, William Kirby, would come with his wife.

And that July night—it was the 7th—the cars raced past as usual along the main road to Deauville. At one in the morning the Pavillon Bleu and the other restaurants and cafés shut their doors.

A motorist, who stopped for a moment near the Hendersons', subsequently informed the police that at about half past two he had seen a light upstairs in the house and shadows silhouetted against the blinds, which struck him as odd.

In the morning, at six, the gardener arrived as he always did on Thursdays. He used to go quietly to work, and then at eight o'clock Élise Chatrier would call him in to have some coffee.

But at eight o'clock there was no sign of life, nor at nine. Becoming anxious, he knocked, and as there was no answer he fetched a policeman.

Then the crime was discovered. In Mrs. Henderson's room the old lady's body was sprawling across the carpet, her nightgown soaked in blood, a dozen knife wounds in her chest.

Élise Chatrier had met the same fate in the next room. Mrs. Henderson liked to have her near her, in case she was taken ill during the night.

A double murder of the most savage kind, a typical example of what the police call a dirty crime.

And traces everywhere. Footprints, bloody finger marks on the curtains, and all over the place.

The usual routine: arrival of the examining magistrate, the police pathologists, photographers, etc. The usual analysis and postmortems.

Maigret was put in charge of the case, and it did not take him long to get on Heurtin's track.

It was so clearly marked. There was no carpet in the passages, and the floors were beeswaxed. The photographs showed imprints of exceptional clarity.

They were of rubber soles, absolutely new. The non-slip ridges were quite distinctive, and the maker's name and a number were clearly legible.

A few hours later Maigret entered a shoe shop in the Boulevard Raspail, where he learned that shoes of that description and size had been sold within the last fortnight.

"Wait a moment. It was a fellow with a trike. We often see him around here."

And a few more hours brought the inspector to the florist's in the Rue de Sèvres, where he questioned Monsieur Gérardier; an hour later he found the shoes themselves on Joseph Heurtin's feet.

It only remained to compare the fingerprints. The experts bent over them with their lenses. Their verdict was immediate:

"That's the chap."

---

"What did you do it for?"

"I didn't kill anybody."

"Who gave you Mrs. Henderson's address?"

"I didn't kill anybody."

"What were you doing in the house at two in the morning?"

"I don't know."

"How did you get back from Saint-Cloud?"

"I didn't get back from Saint-Cloud!"

A large head, pale face, great bumps on the skull. And his eyelids were red, like those of a man who hasn't slept for days and days.

In his room in the Rue Monsieur-le-Prince they found a bloodstained handkerchief, and the experts said it was human blood. And they even found certain bacilli in it that were also in Mrs. Henderson's.

"I didn't kill anybody."

"What lawyer would you like?"

"I don't want a lawyer."

They gave him one all the same, Maître Joly, a young man just turned thirty, who racked his brains to find some kind of defense.

They put him under observation for a week, and the specialists reported:

"No signs of degeneracy. The man is fully responsible for his actions in spite of his present prostration, which is the result of a severe nervous shock."

It was during the summer holidays. Maigret was sent off on a case at Deauville. The examining magistrate, Coméliau, found the case clear enough; so did the Public Prosecutor. But the fact remained that Heurtin had stolen nothing and had apparently nothing whatever to gain by the death of either of the victims.

Maigret had routed out all he could about his past. He could claim to know him morally and physically at every age.

He was born at Melun where his father was a waiter at the Hôtel de la Seine and his mother a washerwoman. Three years later his parents set up on their own with a lit-tle café. But business was not good, and they moved to Nandy in Seine-et-Marne where they started an inn. When Joseph was six, a sister, Odette, was born.

Maigret had a photograph of a naked baby lying on a bearskin, its podgy arms and legs waving in the air, while squatting in the foreground in sailor clothes was Joseph.

At thirteen he was looking after the horses and helping to serve the customers. At seventeen he was a waiter in a smart hotel in Fontainebleau. At twenty-one, having fin-ished his military service, he settled in Paris in the Rue Monsieur-le-Prince and delivered flowers for Monsieur Gérardier.

"He read a lot," said Monsieur Gérardier.

"His only entertainment was to go to the pictures," said his landlady.

But there was nothing that had the least bearing on the house at Saint-Cloud.

"Had you ever been to Saint-Cloud before?"

"Never."

"What did you do on Sundays?"

"I used to read."

Mrs. Henderson was not a customer of Monsieur Gérardier's. There was nothing to attract a burglar to that house rather than to a hundred others. And anyhow, nothing had been stolen.

"Why don't you speak out?"

"I've nothing to say."

For a whole month Maigret was at Deauville, rounding up a gang of international crooks, and it was not till September that he saw Heurtin again in his cell in the Santé. He found him utterly prostrated.

"I don't know anything. I didn't kill anybody."

"But you were at Saint-Cloud all right."

"Leave me alone."

The prosecution thought it plain sailing. The case was listed to open the autumn session of the Seine Assizes on October 1.

Maître Joly had only one line of defense, calling an expert witness to pronounce on the state of Heurtin's mind. And this specialist had said:

"Responsibility subnormal."

To which the prosecution had replied:

"A dirty crime. If the accused didn't steal anything, it was because something cropped up to disturb him. The experts had counted *as many as eighteen knife wounds.*"

They passed around the photographs of the victims, which the jury hardly glanced at, turning away in disgust.

"Yes," to all questions.

Sentence of death. And the next day Joseph Heurtin was transferred to a cell in the Quartier de la Grande Surveillance, where four others were awaiting the same end.

Maigret was annoyed with him.

"You've nothing to say to me?" he asked.

"Nothing."

"You know what you're in for?"

And Heurtin wept quietly, his face pale as ever, his eyes red.

"Who's your accomplice?"

"I haven't got one."

And every day Maigret returned, though strictly speaking he had no longer any right to interfere. Every day he found Heurtin prostrated, but calm. He never trembled, and now and again there was a glint of a sneer in the pupils of his eyes . . .

Until the day when he heard steps in the next cell and piercing shrieks. They had come for No. 9, a parricide.

Next day Heurtin, now No. 11, was sobbing. But still he wouldn't speak. He lay stretched full length on the bed, his face turned to the wall, his teeth chattering.

When Maigret got an idea in his head, it was not easily eradicated. And he went to Coméliau.

"Either he's mad or he's innocent," he said.

"It's impossible. Besides, the case can't be reopened now."

Maigret stood there, five foot eleven, broad-shouldered, powerful. He held his ground.

"You know, we could never find out how he got back from Saint-Cloud to Paris. He didn't go by train. That's proved. Nor by tram. And he certainly didn't walk."

Monsieur Coméliau jeered, but Maigret remained unshaken.

"Would you like to try an experiment?"

"You must ask the Ministry."

And Maigret, weighty, obstinate, went to the Ministry of Justice. He had prepared a note for the condemned man telling him how to get away.

"Look here. If he has accomplices he'll think the message comes from them; if he hasn't he'll be suspicious, thinking it's a trap of some sort. I'll make myself personally responsible for him. I guarantee that whatever happens he won't get out of our clutches."

It was good to see the inspector's face, heavy, placid, and yet hard. And that went on for three days. He played on their feelings by talking of a miscarriage of justice and of the scandal there would be when it one day came to light.

"But it was you who arrested him."

"As a policeman, I am bound to draw the logical conclusion from material evidence."

"And as a man?"

"I want moral proof."

"So you think . . . ?"

"He's either mad or innocent."

"Why doesn't he talk?"

"The experiment I am proposing will answer that
for us."

There were telephone calls and conferences.

"You're risking your career, inspector. Think it over."

"I've thought it over."

And the note was sent. The condemned man didn't
breathe a word about it, and for the last three days he ate
with more appetite.

"You see, he's not surprised," said Maigret. "So he was
expecting something of the sort. In other words, he has accomplices who promised to get him out."

"Unless he's acting . . . And, once outside, there's always a chance of his slipping through your fingers. Don't
forget, your career's at stake, inspector."

"And a man's head."

———————

So here was Maigret lounging in a leather-covered easy
chair by the window of the hotel bedroom. Occasionally he
turned his glasses on the Citanguette where the dockers
and workmen were drifting in for a drink.

On the quay, Janvier was trying hard to look natural

doing nothing. Dufour had been eating an *andouillette* with mashed potatoes—Maigret could see every detail—and was now drinking a calvados.

The window above was still shut.

"Get me the Citanguette, mademoiselle."

"The line's engaged."

"I don't care. Clear it."

And a moment or two later: "Is that you, Dufour?"

"Still sleeping," answered a bored voice.

There was a knock on the door. It was Lucas, who coughed as he made his way through the cloud of pipe smoke.

## THE EVENING PAPER

"Got anything?"

Lucas sat down on the edge of the bed, after touching the inspector's hand.

"Yes, I've got something. But nothing very startling. The editor ended by giving me the letter informing him of the Santé business. It had reached him about ten o'clock."

"Let's see it."

Lucas handed over a dirty piece of paper, heavily scored with blue pencil. For when it had got to the *Sifflet* they had simply crossed out a few passages and made the necessary corrections and sent it straight down to the printers. There were also some typographical instructions and the initials of the linotype operator who had set it up.

"A bit of notepaper with the top cut off," observed Maigret. "No doubt to get rid of a printed heading."

"Exactly. I thought so at once, and I thought it would most likely have been written in a café. I took it to Moers, who claims to know the notepaper of most of the cafés in Paris."

"Could he spot it?"

"It didn't take him ten minutes. This sheet came from

the Coupole in the Boulevard Montparnasse. I've just been round there. Unfortunately they have a thousand customers a day if they have one, and at least fifty ask for writing materials."

"What does Moers say of the writing?"

"He wouldn't say anything. Wants to have it back to study properly. In the meantime, if you'd like me to go back to the Coupole . . ."

But Maigret was staring at the Citanguette. The gates of the neighboring factory had been flung open to a stream of workmen, most of them cycling, who gradually disappeared into the gray twilight.

The bar of the Citanguette was lit up by a single electric lamp, by the light of which the inspector could see the customers inside.

There were half a dozen of them at the zinc counter, and one or two of them were looking at Dufour rather suspiciously. Maigret passed the glasses to Lucas, who exclaimed a moment later:

"Hallo! What's he doing there? And isn't that Janvier on the quay watching the water go by?"

Maigret did not answer. He took the glasses back and gazed through them. He could see the staircase, which ended in a spiral just behind the counter. And on it at that moment two legs came into view. They stopped, then continued. Finally a figure came forward and the light shone on the pale face of Joseph Heurtin.

At the same moment Maigret noticed an evening paper that had just been thrown onto one of the tables.

"By the way, Lucas, do you know if the other evening papers have got that stuff from the *Sifflet*?"

"I haven't seen any, but I should think they're bound to, if only to annoy us."

Maigret lifted the receiver again.

"The Citanguette, mademoiselle, and as quick as you can."

For the first time since the morning, Maigret was feverish. On the other side of the Seine the landlord was speaking to Heurtin, presumably asking him what he would drink.

Wouldn't the fugitive's first thought be to look at the paper lying there within reach of his hand?

"Hallo! hallo! Yes. Ask him to speak to me at once."

He could see Dufour get up and go into the call box.

"Look here, old man. There's a paper lying on the table there. He must not read it. *On no account . . .*"

"Shall I . . . ?" but Maigret interrupted him.

"Quick! He's just sitting down. The paper's right under his nose."

Maigret was on his feet, all his muscles contracted. If Heurtin read that article it would be all up with the scheme he had so laboriously concocted.

He could see Heurtin sit down on the seat against the wall, putting his two elbows on the table and taking his head in his hands.

The proprietor came up and placed a drink before him. Dufour was coming back to take the paper.

Lucas, though he did not know the details of the case,

guessed what was afoot, and strained his eyes to try to follow what was happening. For a moment their view was obstructed by a tug that had just lit up its navigation lights, white, red, green, and was swinging around in the stream, blowing its siren wildly.

"That's torn it," groaned Maigret as Heurtin casually took up the paper, just as Dufour had nearly crossed the room. If the news was there, it would surely be on the front page. Would it catch his eye at once?

And would Dufour have enough presence of mind to deal with the situation?

Dufour came nearer, but—how typical!—before acting he couldn't help casting a look across the Seine toward the hotel from where his chief was watching him.

Certainly he didn't look the right man for the job. So small and neat, there in a bar jostling with rough dockhands and workmen from the factory.

Nevertheless, he went straight up to Heurtin, holding out his hand. He must be saying:

"Pardon, monsieur, that's my paper."

The men at the counter turned around. Heurtin looked up at the detective with astonishment.

Dufour insisted, leaning over the table and taking hold of the paper. Lucas peered harder than ever, holding his breath. It was indeed the critical moment.

Heurtin got up slowly, like a man who does not yet know what he's going to do. His left hand still gripped the newspaper, while Dufour did not let go of it either.

Suddenly Heurtin's free hand seized a siphon that was

standing on the next table, and the thick heavy glass came down on the detective's skull.

Janvier, by the riverside, was barely fifty yards away. But he heard nothing.

Dufour staggered back against the counter, breaking two glasses. Two men caught hold of his arms, while three others rushed at Heurtin. There must have been a bit of a hubbub, for Janvier at last stopped contemplating the lights reflected in the water. He turned his head sharply toward the Citanguette, and started walking toward it, then breaking into a run.

"Quick! Take a taxi," said Maigret. "Get there as fast as you can."

Lucas obeyed without enthusiasm. He knew he'd be too late. Even Janvier, who was on the spot . . .

Heurtin was struggling. He seemed to be shouting out something. Was he accusing Dufour of being a policeman? Anyhow they let go of him for a moment, and he took advantage of his freedom to have a swipe at the electric light with the siphon he was still holding in his hand.

Maigret stood motionless, his two hands clenched on the railing that ran across outside the tall French windows. On the quay below a taxi started off. A match was struck in the Citanguette, but it instantly went out again. In spite of the distance, Maigret was almost sure he heard a shot.

———————

Interminable minutes. The taxi was across the bridge now, trundling along the rutty track along the other bank of the

Seine. It was so slow that, when he was still two hundred yards from the Citanguette, Lucas jumped out and started running. Perhaps he had heard the shot.

A whistle blew. Lucas or Janvier summoning help. A candle was lit in the bar, lighting up the dirty windows on one of which was a notice in white enamel letters, telling customers they could bring their own food: *On peut apporter son manger*, from which the M and the last R were missing. It also showed a group of figures bending over a form on the floor.

But the light was too dim, the figures too indistinct for Maigret to recognize them at that distance. With his eyes still glued to the Citanguette, he telephoned again. His voice had gone toneless.

"Hallo! Grenelle Police? Send some men quickly by car to surround the Citanguette. And if he tries to get away, arrest a tall man with a large head and pale face. And send for a doctor."

Lucas was in the building now. The taxi had followed him and was drawn up in front of one of the windows, hiding part of the scene from Maigret's view.

Standing on a chair, the landlord put in a fresh electric bulb, and the place was once more bathed in crude light.

The telephone rang in Maigret's room.

"Hallo! Is that you, inspector? Coméliau speaking. I'm ringing up from home. We've got people coming to dinner. And I just wanted to make sure . . ."

Maigret said nothing.

"Hallo! Don't cut me off. Are you there?"

"Yes."

"Well? . . . I can hardly hear you. Have you seen the papers? They've all got the *Sifflet* story. I think we ought perhaps to . . ."

Janvier ran out of the Citanguette and dashed around the corner to the right, disappearing into the darkness.

"But apart from that," went on Coméliau, "everything's all right, I suppose?"

"Everything's all right," said Maigret, and he rang off.

He was sweating all over. His pipe had fallen on the floor and some glowing tobacco was burning the carpet.

"Hallo! The Citanguette, please, mademoiselle."

"But I've just given you your number."

"I said the Citanguette. Get it."

He could see their heads turn as the telephone rang over on the other side. The landlord went to answer it, but Lucas pushed in front of him.

"Is that you, inspector?"

"Yes," said Maigret dully. "He's got away, hasn't he?"

"Naturally."

"And Dufour?"

"I don't think it's serious. A scalp wound. He wasn't even knocked out."

"I've called out the Grenelle Police."

"They won't do any good. You know what it's like over here. All these wharves with their stacks of goods, then the factories, and the little lanes of Issy-les-Moulineaux . . ."

"Did somebody shoot?"

"There was a shot. But I can't make out who fired it. They're all bewildered here, quiet as lambs. They can't make out what's going on."

A car appeared. Two policemen got out. Another two were dropped a hundred yards farther on. Lastly four got out at the Citanguette, one making straight for the rear to guard the back door, following the usual routine.

"What shall I do?" asked Lucas.

"Nothing. Oh, well: organize a search, just in case . . . I'm coming around."

"What about a doctor?"

"I've seen to that."

---

The girl in reception, who also saw to the telephone, quailed before the big man looking down on her. He was icy calm, Maigret, his face so shut, so stony that it did not seem to be made of flesh at all.

"The bill, please."

"You're going?"

"The bill, please."

"I shall have to ask the manageress. How many telephone calls did you have? Just wait a moment, please . . ."

She got up from her chair, but Maigret seized her by the arm and sat her down again. Then, putting a hundred-franc note on the desk, he asked:

"Is that enough?"

"I suppose so . . . Yes . . . But . . ."

He went out with a sigh, and walked along the pavement and over the bridge, with a slow stride that never quickened for a moment.

He tapped his pockets, feeling for his pipe, but it was not there. No doubt he regarded it as an evil omen, for his lips puckered for a moment into a bitter smile.

There were a few watermen around the Citanguette, but they did not seem unduly interested by what was going on. The previous week, two Arabs had knifed each other at the same place, and, a month before that, a sack containing the trunk and legs of a woman had been fished out of the water with a boat hook.

The smart flats of Auteuil formed the horizon of the other bank of the Seine. A metro train roared by over one of the bridges. It was drizzling. Uniformed policemen came and went, turning their pale electric torches this way and that.

Lucas was the only man standing in the bar. The men who had witnessed or taken part in the scuffle were seated in a row against the wall. He went from one to the other of them, examining their papers, while sour looks were turned on him.

Dufour had already been taken off in the police car, which was driven over the rough road as gently as possible.

Maigret said nothing. With his hands stuffed in his overcoat pockets, he just stood there looking about him with an eye that seemed immeasurably heavy.

The landlord started on an explanation:

"I swear, inspector, I didn't . . ."

Maigret shut him up with a stare and turned to an Arab sitting on the bench. The man went putty-colored as the inspector looked him over from head to foot.

"So you've got a job now?"

"At Citroën's, yes, . . . I . . ."

"For how much longer are you forbidden to be in the district?"

And Maigret made a sign to one of the policemen that meant:

"Off with him!"

"Inspector," whined the Arab as he was led toward the door, "let me explain . . . I haven't done anything . . ."

But Maigret took no notice. There was a Pole whose papers were not in order:

"Off with him!"

That was all. On the floor they found Dufour's revolver with a cartridge fired, the siphon, and splinters of glass from the lamp. The newspaper was torn, and two drops of blood had splashed onto it.

"What shall we do with this lot?" asked Lucas, who had done looking at their papers.

"Let 'em go."

A quarter of an hour later Janvier came back. He found Maigret sunk in a chair in a corner of the bar. Lucas was sitting near him. Janvier's boots and trousers were muddy, and there were dirty marks on his mackintosh.

There was nothing to say. He sat down with the others. Maigret's thoughts seemed far away. The landlord stood behind the counter, looking very humble and contrite. Staring vaguely in his direction Maigret said:

"Some rum."

And once again he felt for his pipe.

"Give me a cigarette," he said to Janvier with a sigh.

Janvier tried hard to find something to say. But he was too upset by the sight of his chief's hunched shoulders to think of anything. He blew his nose and looked away.

Meanwhile the examining magistrate, Monsieur Coméliau, sat at the head of a table laid for twenty. After dinner there was to be dancing.

As for Dufour, he was lying on a steel table at a doctor's in Grenelle. The latter slipped on a white overall while his instruments were being sterilized.

"Will it show?" asked the policeman, who could see nothing but the ceiling. "The skull's not broken, is it?"

"Good gracious, no. Nothing at all. Just a matter of a few stitches."

"And the hair will grow again? Really? You're quite sure?"

# 4

# HEADQUARTERS

Maigret listened stolidly. He never once made the least sign of protest or impatience.

With grave face and drawn features he listened humbly, respectfully, right to the end: only just a little quiver of the Adam's apple at those passages that contained Monsieur Coméliau's most pungent strictures.

Thin, nervous, exasperated, the examining magistrate paced up and down his room. Sometimes his voice rose almost to a shout so that his words were even audible to the people waiting outside in the corridor.

Now and again he would pick up some object from his desk, fiddle with it for a few moments, then fling it down again. The clerk, embarrassed, looked the other way. And Maigret stood there, steadily, towering above the angry little man.

The latter, after a final jibe, looked into the inspector's face. But he quickly turned his head away; for after all Maigret was a man of forty-five who for over twenty years had been in the police, handling all sorts of cases, many of them extremely delicate.

And then . . . Well, he was a man!

"But haven't you anything to say?"

"I told my chief just now that I'll hand in my resignation in ten days' time if I don't lay hands on the murderer."

"In other words, if you don't lay hands on Joseph Heurtin . . ."

"Lay hands on the murderer," said Maigret simply.

The examining magistrate flared up again.

"Do you mean to tell me you still believe . . . ?"

Maigret said nothing, and Coméliau, writhing with impatience, hastily added:

"Let's leave it at that, or you'll end by driving me out of my mind. As soon as you've anything to report, ring me up."

Maigret took his leave and made his way along the familiar corridors. But, instead of going down to the street, he climbed up to the top floor of the Palais de Justice, where he pushed open the door of the laboratory of the Police Scientifique.

One of the experts, suddenly seeing him, was so struck by his appearance that, as he held out his hand, he asked:

"Aren't you well?"

"Quite all right, thanks."

His eyes seemed to look at nothing. He kept his heavy black overcoat on, his hands in the pockets. He looked like someone who has returned from a long journey and is seeing a familiar spot with fresh eyes.

Nor did his manner change as he started to turn over some photographs taken the day before in a flat that had been burgled. Then he read a report that one of his colleagues had asked for.

Over in a corner was a hairless young man, tall and weedy. He was shortsighted and wore thick-lensed glasses. He was watching Maigret with a look of pained surprise.

On his table were lenses of all shapes and sizes, delicate tools, bottles of ink, and chemical reagents, also a screen of frosted glass that was lit up by a powerful electric lamp.

It was Moers, the specialist on papers, inks, and handwriting. He knew Maigret had come to see him, but the latter did not even look at him as he wandered aimlessly about the room.

At last he took out his pipe, lit it, and in a strained voice said:

"Well, now! Let's get to work."

Moers understood—he knew where the inspector came from—but he pretended not to notice.

Maigret took off his coat, yawned, worked the muscles of his face, as though to regain his normal self. He seized a chair, took it over to the young man and sat astride of it, leaning over the back. In an affectionate tone he said:

"Well, little chap?"

Some of the weight at least seemed to have fallen from his shoulders.

"Tell me all you can."

"I spent last night studying the note. A pity it's been mauled by so many people. Not the faintest use looking for fingerprints."

"No. I didn't expect any."

"I called at the Coupole first thing this morning and examined all the ink pots. Do you know the place? There are several rooms: the big one, part of which is turned into a restaurant at mealtimes, then the one on the first floor; then there's the terrace, and lastly a small place on the left, an American bar frequented chiefly by habitués."

"I know."

"Well, it was the ink belonging to that bar that was used to write the letter. The writing was done with the left hand, not by a left-handed person, but by somebody who knew that all left-handed writings look very much alike."

The letter that had been sent to the *Sifflet* still lay on the glass screen in front of Moers.

"One thing is certain: the writer is an intellectual, and I could swear to it that he speaks and writes several languages. But of course if I'm going to give you a portrait of him—that's not strict science, you know."

"Go on."

"Well, either I'm very much mistaken or we're dealing with an exceptional person. First of all, an intelligence far above the average. But what bothers me is the strange mixture of willpower and weakness, also of coldness and emotional capacity. It's a man's writing, yet I can see various traits that are definitely feminine."

Moers was on his favorite ground. He positively glowed with pleasure. In spite of himself, Maigret could not help smiling slightly, and the young man hastily went on:

"Of course, I know all that's not very convincing, and

an examining magistrate would never hear me out . . . All the same . . . for instance, I'd bet anything you like that the man who wrote that letter is the victim of a serious illness. And he knows it . . . If only he'd written with the right hand, I could have told you more . . . Oh, I'd forgotten— there are stains on the paper, though of course they might have been done at the printer's. One of those spots is certainly *café au lait*. And one more thing—the top of the sheet was not cut off with a knife, but with something rounded, like a spoon."

"In short, the letter was written yesterday morning in the bar of the Coupole by a polyglot customer who was probably drinking a *café-crème*."

Maigret got up and offered his hand.

"Thank you, my boy. Give me back the letter, will you?"

He grunted a general farewell and went out. When the door was shut someone said, though not without a certain admiration:

"He's got it in the neck, if ever . . ."

But Moers, who was well known as a Maigret fan, glared at him, and the man stopped and went on with his analysis.

————

Paris wore its dismal mid-October aspect. A raw light fell from a sky that was like a dirty ceiling. The pavements still showed traces of the previous night's rain. And the passers-by had the resentful look of people who were not yet used to the idea that summer was over.

Throughout the night police typewriters had been busy at the Préfecture. Orders had been distributed by hand to all the Paris police stations. Messages had been telegraphed all over the country telling gendarmes, railway police, and customs officers to be on the lookout.

High and low, from one end of Paris to the other and in all the surrounding suburbs, uniformed men and plainclothes detectives were on the prowl, scrutinizing every face in the hope of setting hands on a certain man. The same in the suburbs. In the country travelers on the main roads were stopped and asked for their papers. At the frontiers people were surprised at being questioned more minutely than usual.

They were after Joseph Heurtin, condemned to death at the Seine Assizes, escaped from the Santé, and who had disappeared after a scuffle with a detective in a bar called the Citanguette.

"At the moment of his flight from the Citanguette he had about twenty-two francs left in his pocket," said the information that had been circulated.

And Maigret's solitary figure walked away from the Palais de Justice. But, instead of going to his office on the Quai des Orfèvres, he took a bus to the Bastille, and rang the bell of a third-floor flat in the Rue du Chemin-Vert.

The door was opened by Madame Dufour. Still busy with the housework, she had not yet had time to dress. A smell of some surgical disinfectant mingled with that of boiled fowl.

"Ah! He will be pleased to see you," she said.

In his room the detective was lying in bed, looking sad and worried.

"Getting on, old man?"

"I suppose so. It seems, after all, that the hair won't grow over the scar. I shall be lucky if I don't have to wear a wig."

Maigret wandered around the room, as he had at the laboratory, like a man who doesn't know what to be at. Finally he muttered:

"Have you got a grudge against me?"

Dufour's wife, still young and pretty, was standing in the doorway.

"I'd like to see him having a grudge against you!" she said. "All the morning he's been saying he wondered how you were going to pull through. He wanted me to go to the post office to ring you up, as our line's out of order this morning."

"Oh, don't worry. Things will straighten themselves out somehow or other," answered Maigret.

His own home was only five hundred yards away, in the Boulevard Richard Lenoir, but he did not go there. He started to walk. That's what he needed—to walk, to feel himself in the middle of the crowd that jostled him, indifferent to his cares.

Little by little, as he made his way through the streets, he lost the look of a guilty schoolboy. His features grew firmer. He smoked pipe after pipe, as in his best days.

Monsieur Coméliau would have been astonished, and no doubt indignant, had he known that the least of the inspector's worries was to recapture Joseph Heurtin.

For Maigret, that was a minor question. The escaped man was somewhere or other among a crowd of many millions. But Maigret felt pretty sure that, the day he needed him, he would put his hand on him almost at once.

No. His thoughts were centered on the letter written in the Coupole. And also, perhaps even more, on a question that he was annoyed with himself for having neglected at the time.

But in July everybody was so sure of Heurtin's guilt. Coméliau had taken the case in hand at once, thus eliminating the police.

The crime was committed at Saint-Cloud at about two o'clock in the morning. Heurtin was back in the Rue Monsieur-le-Prince before four. He didn't go by train, nor by tram, nor in fact by any public means of conveyance. Neither did he take a taxi. And his trike remained at his employer's in the Rue de Sèvres.

And he couldn't have got back on foot. At least, unless he'd run the whole way without stopping.

In the Boulevard Montparnasse was the usual midday animation. It was half past twelve. In spite of the late-autumn weather, the terraces of the four big cafés near the Boulevard Raspail were packed with people, eighty percent of whom were foreigners.

Maigret crossed to the Coupole, and went into the American bar.

There were only five tables there, all of them occupied. Most of the customers were perched on the high stools at the counter or standing about.

He heard someone call out:

"A Manhattan."

And he said: "The same for me."

He was not himself of the cocktail generation. Beer was more in his line. The barman pushed a dish of olives toward him, but he did not touch them.

"Excuse me . . ." said a little Swedish girl with very yellow hair.

The place was writhing with humanity. A trap at the end of the room opened and shut ceaselessly, disgorging olives, chips, sandwiches, hot drinks.

Four waiters were all shouting at once, accompanied by the clatter of plates and tinkling of glasses. Snatches of different languages broke in on all sides. Yet somehow the whole scene—customers, barmen, waiters, the room itself— gave the impression of a homogeneous whole.

People jostled one another without ceremony; and everybody called the head barman Bob. Everybody: chorus girls, penniless artists, or industrial magnates who drove up with their friends in luxurious cars.

People accosted each other without introduction. A German was speaking English with a Yankee, while a Norwegian was making use of at least three languages to make himself understood to a Spaniard.

There were two women who seemed to be known to all. Everybody greeted them. One of them Maigret recognized. She had aged and grown stout, but there was no doubt: she was the same girl he had once had to take to Saint-Lazare after a raid in the Rue de la Roquette.

Her voice was husky, her eyes tired, though she certainly looked prosperous in her furs. She shook hands casually with people as they passed. Sitting at one of the tables she seemed to be enthroned, and tacitly accepted as the matriarch of that boisterous family around her.

"Have you got anything I can write with?" asked Maigret of one of the barmen.

"Not at this time of day. Too busy here with the cocktails, but they'll see to you next door."

Among the chattering groups there were, however, one or two people who were quite by themselves, making a contrast with the others that was not the least picturesque feature of the place.

On the one hand, people shouting at the tops of their voices and ordering round after round of drinks, people whose clothes were as eccentric as they were costly. On the other, a few beings who seemed to have come from the four corners of the earth for no better purpose than to sit there embedded in that smart crowd, without saying a word to anybody.

For instance, there was a girl who could hardly have been much more than twenty, dressed in a little coat and skirt that was well cut but had certainly been pressed a hundred times. A queer face, tired and nervous. By her side was a sketchbook. And in the middle of those people drinking cocktails at ten francs a time she was drinking a glass of milk and eating a croissant. At one o'clock—so it was obviously her midday meal. She was taking the opportunity to read a Russian paper that was provided for the customers.

She heard nothing and saw nothing. Slowly she munched her croissant, taking a sip of milk from time to time, ignoring the others at her table, who were now at their fourth round.

No less striking was a man with a head of hair that was alone sufficient to attract attention. It was red, frizzy, and very long. He wore a dark suit, shiny and threadbare, with an open-necked blue shirt.

He had installed himself at the extreme end of the bar, and looked like an old habitué that no one would think of disturbing. Spoonful by spoonful, he was eating a pot of yogurt.

Had he as much as five francs in his pocket? Where did he come from? What was he after? And how did he come by the few sous he needed to pay for that yogurt, which was probably his only meal that day? Like the Russian girl, he had keen eyes under tired lids, but there was also something infinitely haughty and contemptuous in his expression.

No one shook hands with him in passing. No one spoke to him.

The revolving doors suddenly swept a couple into the bar, and Maigret, catching sight of them in a mirror, at once recognized the Kirbys.

They had driven there in an American car that could

not have been bought in Paris for less than 250,000 francs at the very lowest estimate. It stood there by the curb, the more noticeable for the fact that its body was completely chromium-plated.

And William Kirby, pushing his way between two people, held out a hand across the mahogany bar.

"How are you, Bob?"

Mrs. Kirby went straight up to the yellow-haired Swedish girl, kissing her and talking volubly in English.

The newcomers had no need to order drinks. Bob promptly handed Kirby a whiskey and soda, and mixed a Rose for his young wife, asking:

"Back from Biarritz already?"

"Only stayed there three days. It was raining worse than here."

Kirby caught sight of Maigret and nodded. He was a tall, dark, supple man, about thirty. He was impeccably dressed. In fact of all those people gathered there, he was perhaps the one in whom style was least flashy.

He shook hands with his friends casually, rather too softly, asking them:

"What'll you have?"

He was rich. With that sports car outside, he would dash off to Nice, Biarritz, Deauville, or Berlin just when it took his fancy.

He had been living in a grand hotel in the Avenue George V for the last few years, and from his aunt, the murdered woman, he had inherited the house at Saint-Cloud and fifteen or twenty million francs.

Mrs. Kirby was small and fragile, but extremely lively. She talked without stopping in a high-pitched voice by which you could have picked her out anywhere. She spoke a mixture of English and French, the latter with an amazing accent.

People were standing between them and Maigret. A deputy came in, cordially shaking Kirby's hand.

"Shall we lunch together?"

"Not today. We go on to some friends."

"Tomorrow then?"

"Right. Meet us here."

"Monsieur Valanchine!" called a page boy. "Telephone call for Monsieur Valanchine!" Someone got up hurriedly.

"Two Roses, two!" called another.

More clatter of plates. The noise seemed to increase every minute.

"Can you change me some dollars?" And then the same voice:

"You can find the rate of exchange in the paper."

"Isn't Suzy here?"

"She's just gone out. Has a lunch at Maxim's."

Maigret, for his part, was thinking of the young man with the queer-shaped head and long arms, who at that very moment was somewhere or other in this teeming city with just over twenty francs in his pocket, hunted by the whole police of France.

He thought of the pale splodge of his face against the dark wall of the Santé as he had slowly hauled himself up.

And then Dufour's report over the telephone:

"Still sleeping."

He had slept the whole day long.

Where was he now? And why should he have killed that Mrs. Henderson whom he had never known and from whom he had stolen nothing?

"Do you drop in here for a cocktail sometimes?"

It was William Kirby, who had come up to Maigret and was now holding out his cigarette case.

"No, thanks. I only smoke a pipe."

"Well, have a drink? Whiskey?"

"I've got one already."

Kirby looked a trifle put out.

"You can follow these languages? English, Russian, German?"

"Only French, that's all."

"Then this place must seem rather a Babel to you. I don't think I've ever noticed you here . . . By the way, is it true, what they say?"

"What do you mean?"

"That the murderer . . . You know . . ."

"Oh, that's nothing to worry about."

For a moment Kirby looked him in the face.

"Come on. Do join us and have a drink. My wife would be so pleased. And let me introduce you to Miss Edna Reichberg. Her father's the paper manufacturer of Stockholm. She won the skating championship last year at Chamonix. Here, Edna, this is Inspector Maigret: Miss Reichberg."

The Russian girl in the black coat and skirt was still

deep in her newspaper, and the red-haired man was staring dreamily through half-closed eyes. Before him was the empty little earthenware pot from which he had laboriously scraped the last scrap of yogurt.

"Delighted," said Edna, shaking Maigret's hand heartily, then turning back to Mrs. Kirby and going on with her conversation in English.

"Excuse me," said William. "I'm wanted on the telephone. Two whiskeys, Bob. You don't mind, do you?"

Outside, the chromium-plated car glittered in the dull gray light, while a pathetic figure was wandering about in front of it. He shuffled toward the bar, dragging his feet, and stopped for a moment at the door.

Two red-rimmed eyes stared into the bar. A waiter made toward the door, ready to turn him away.

In Paris and elsewhere the police were still looking for the man who had escaped from the Santé.

And there he was, almost within speaking distance of the inspector!

# 5

# CAVIAR SANDWICHES

Maigret did not move a muscle. Beside him Mrs. Kirby and the Swedish girl went on babbling in English over their cocktails. And so close was he to the latter, packed tight as they all were in that crowded bar, that he was conscious of every movement of her supple body.

He could not of course follow their conversation, but it seemed to be about a certain José, whom Edna had met at the Ritz and who had flirted with her and offered her cocaine.

The two women laughed. William Kirby returned, saying to Maigret:

"So sorry, but it was about that car of mine. I want to sell it and get another."

He squirted soda water into the two glasses.

"Cheers!"

Outside, the figure of the condemned man seemed literally to float about the precincts of the café. He was bareheaded, having lost his cap, no doubt, in his flight from the Citanguette. His head had been cropped in prison, which exaggerated still more the size of his ears. His boots had no longer any color or shape.

And where could he have slept to have got his suit so crumpled and covered with dust and mud?

If he had held out his hand to beg, it would have seemed quite natural, for he looked utterly derelict. But he didn't beg, nor had he any bootlaces or pencils to sell.

He went this way and that way, carried hither and thither by the ebb and flow of the crowd. When he was swept a little distance away, he would drag himself back like a man fighting his way upstream.

His face was dark with some days' growth of beard. He looked thinner. But his eyes were haunting: eyes that never lost sight of the American bar, and tried from time to time to peer in through the misty windows.

Once again he came right up to the door, and it almost looked as though he was going to push it open.

Maigret smoked furiously, his temples moist with sweat, his nerves keyed up to a pitch that doubled the sharpness of his senses.

It was an extraordinary transformation. A little earlier he had looked a beaten man. He had lost his foothold. The threads of the drama had slipped from his grasp and he had no reason to suppose he would ever gather them up again.

He sipped his whiskey. Kirby was talking with the two women, though constantly turning to Maigret to include him politely in the conversation.

It was strange: without making the smallest effort and almost unconscious of his perspicuity, Maigret missed nothing of what was going on. People were bustling and buzzing all round him. The noises were so many and various that they fused into a vague roar like that of the sea.

Voices, movements, attitudes—nothing escaped him. He watched the man sitting over the empty pot of yogurt, and the vagabond who was so irresistibly attracted by that door. He saw Kirby's smile, his wife's pout as she rouged her lips, the vigorous movements of the barman as he shook a cocktail.

And the customers, now drifting out one by one, arranging to meet again:

"Shall we see you this evening?"

"Try to bring Léa . . ."

Gradually the bar emptied. It had gone half past one. From the next room came the scrape of knives and forks. Kirby put a hundred-franc note on the counter.

"Are you staying?" he asked Maigret.

He hadn't seen the man outside. But he was sure to run right into him as he went out. Maigret waited for it to happen in a suspense that was almost painful. Mrs. Kirby and Edna bowed to him and smiled.

And there he was, Joseph Heurtin, hardly a couple of paces from the door. One of his bootlaces had gone completely. At any moment a policeman might come up to him and tell him to move on, or even ask to see his papers.

The door turned. Kirby, bare-headed, walked across to the car. The two women followed, laughing at a joke.

And nothing happened. Nothing at all. Heurtin took no more notice of the Americans than of any other passers-by.

Nor did Kirby or his wife pay the least attention to him. The three got into the car and slammed the door.

Others left, driving back the vagrant who had come right up to the entrance again.

Then suddenly in one of the mirrors Maigret caught sight of a face. Two bright eyes under thick eyebrows, a smile, such a slight smile, but full of sarcasm.

The lids dropped at once over the too eloquent eyes. But not quickly enough, and the inspector could not help feeling that that sarcastic smile had been for him.

The man who had looked at him, and who now looked at nothing and nobody, was the red-haired customer with the yogurt.

————

When an Englishman who had been reading *The Times* went, no one except Maigret was left on the stools at the bar. Bob announced:

"I'll get my lunch now."

His two assistants were clearing up, collecting empty glasses and what remained of the olives and chips, and wiping the counter.

Only two people were left now, sitting at the tables, the red-haired man and the Russian girl in black. They both seemed quite unconscious of their solitude.

Joseph Heurtin was still wandering up and down outside. His eyes were so lifeless and his face so white that one of the waiters, looking through the window, said to Maigret:

"There's another! Sure to have an epileptic fit or something. They always manage to choose the terrace of a café. I'll send the boy . . ."

"No."

The yogurt man could hear every word, but Maigret hardly lowered his voice to say:

"Ring up the Police Judiciaire for me. Tell them to send someone here, preferably Lucas or Janvier. Got that! Lucas or Janvier."

"For that wretch outside?"

"Never mind."

How quiet it was after the mayhem of a little while ago!

The red-haired man had not betrayed the slightest interest in what Maigret had said. The girl in black turned over the pages of her newspaper.

The second waiter was looking at Maigret inquisitively. And so the minutes went by, trickled by, drop by drop, second by second.

They made up the cash. There was a rustling of banknotes and clink of coins. The waiter who had been to telephone came back.

"They said they'd see to it."

"Thanks."

Maigret's stool creaked under his weight as he sat there smoking pipe after pipe. He emptied his glass, absentmindedly forgetting he had had nothing to eat.

"Coffee."

The order came from the corner: "*Un café-crème.*" It

was the yogurt man. The waiter shrugged his shoulders
with a look at Maigret as he shouted at the trap behind the
counter:

"*Un crème . . . Un . . .*"

And aside he whispered:

"That'll last him till seven o'clock. He's as bad as the
other one there." And he indicated the Russian girl with a
jerk of his head.

Twenty minutes went by. Heurtin, tired of walking
about, was standing stock-still on the curb. A man getting
into a car took him for a beggar and held out a coin, which
the other didn't dare refuse.

Had he anything left of those twenty-something
francs? Had he had anything to eat since the day before?
Had he managed to get any sleep?

The American bar attracted him irresistibly. Once
more he approached, watching for the waiters, who had
already turned him away more than once.

It was the slack time of the day on the terrace, and this
time he reached the place unmolested. His face came right
against the window, his nose flattened absurdly against it,
while his little eyes peered into the bar.

The red-haired man lifted his cup to his lips. He didn't
turn toward the street.

But why should that same smile make his eyes sparkle
once again?

One of the page boys of the café—a boy not yet
sixteen—went up to the ragged creature outside, who

shuffled off once more. Lucas got out of a taxi and came in with a puzzled look. Still more puzzled, he looked about him in the almost empty bar.

"Oh! It's you who . . . ?"

"What'll you have?"

And in a lower voice:

"Look outside."

It took Lucas a few moments to spot the waiting figure. Then his face lit up.

"*Par exemple!* So you've managed to . . ."

"Nothing of the kind. Barman, some cognac."

The Russian girl said with a strong accent:

"Waiter, get me the *Illustration.* And the Professional Directory too."

"Drink it up, old man, and get outside. You won't lose sight of him, will you?"

"Don't you think it might be better . . . ?" And Lucas's hand felt in his pocket, obviously for the handcuffs.

"Not yet. Run along."

Maigret was outwardly calm, but his nerves were so taut that he nearly crushed the glass from which he was drinking.

The red-haired man showed no inclination to go. He sat on, without reading or writing, or looking at anything in particular. And Joseph Heurtin was still prowling around outside.

At four o'clock the situation was exactly the same, with the only difference being that the escaped prisoner had now found a seat and was sitting down, though without taking his eyes off the door of the bar. Maigret had forced himself to eat a sandwich.

The Russian girl, after a long, careful application of makeup, went out, leaving only Maigret and the yogurt man. Heurtin saw the girl go without betraying the faintest interest.

A man put some fresh bottles on the shelf behind the bar. Another gave the floor a hasty sweep. The lights were switched on in the bar, though the streetlamps were not yet lit.

The ring of a spoon against a cup, particularly coming from the corner where the red-haired man was sitting, surprised the barman no less than Maigret.

Without stopping what he was doing, without even troubling to conceal his contempt for so poor a customer, the waiter called out:

"A yogurt and a *café-crème*. Three, and one fifty. Four francs fifty."

"Excuse me . . . Bring me some caviar sandwiches."

The voice was calm, but Maigret could see the eyes laughing under their half-closed lids.

The barman called through the trap:

"A caviar sandwich. One."

"Three," corrected the stranger.

"Three caviars. Three."

The barman looked mistrustfully at his customer, inquiring sarcastically:

"Some vodka too?"

"Yes. Some vodka too."

Maigret was making a frantic effort to understand what was going on. The man had altered. He had lost his look of indifference.

"And some cigarettes," he rapped out.

"Marylands?"

"No, Abdullas."

He smoked one while they made his sandwiches. He scribbled with a pencil on the box. Then he swallowed down the sandwiches so quickly that the waiter's back was hardly turned before he had finished. Then he got up to go.

"Thirty francs, the sandwiches. The vodka, six. The Abdullas, twenty-two. With what you had before, that makes . . ."

"I'll come back and pay you tomorrow."

Maigret was frowning. He could still see Heurtin sitting on the seat.

"Just a moment, please! You can tell that to the manager."

The red-haired man bowed, then sat down again and waited. The manager, in a dinner jacket, arrived on the scene.

"What's the matter?"

"This gentleman here wants to come back and pay tomorrow. Three caviar sandwiches, Abdulla cigarettes, vodka . . ."

The man who was causing the trouble showed no embarrassment whatever. More sarcastic than ever, he merely bowed again, to confirm the waiter's story.

"You've no money on you?"

"Only just enough for the yogurt and the coffee."

"Do you live in the neighbourhood? I could send a man with you . . ."

"I've no money at home."

"Yet you feed on caviar!"

The manager clapped his hands, and a boy in uniform ran up.

"Go and fetch a policeman."

It all happened very quietly. There was no sort of a row.

"You're quite sure you've no money?"

"I think that's what I said."

The boy, who had waited for the answer, now dashed off. Maigret remained impassive. As for the manager, he stood there calmly staring out of the window at the traffic in the Boulevard Montparnasse.

The barman, while polishing up his bottles, threw an understanding look at Maigret from time to time.

In less than three minutes two policemen arrived on bicycles, with the boy at their heels. They parked their machines and came in.

One of them recognized the inspector and was going up to him, but Maigret gave him a look that said:

"Don't drag me into this."

And the manager, without any needless excitement, explained the situation.

"This gentleman ordered caviar, vodka, and expensive cigarettes, and now he says he can't pay."

"I've no money," repeated the red-haired man.

At a sign from Maigret, the policeman confined himself
to saying:

"All right. You can explain things at the Commissariat.
Come with us."

"Won't you have something while you're here?" offered
the manager.

"No, thank you."

Trams and cars followed each other along the Boulevard, and crowds of people hurried past in the misty gray
twilight. The arrested man stopped to light another cigarette before going, and then waved a friendly farewell to
the barman. Lastly his eyes fell on Maigret and dwelled on
him for two or three seconds.

"Come on. Get going. And no funny business, do you
understand?"

The three went out, and the manager walked up to
the bar.

"Isn't that the Czech that had to be thrown out the
other day?"

"That's the fellow," answered the barman. "He sits here
from eight in the morning till eight at night. And we're doing remarkably well if he orders two coffees and a yogurt
in the whole twelve hours."

Maigret had gone to the door and could see Joseph
Heurtin get up from his seat and stand facing the two policemen and the man who had so suddenly taken a fancy to
caviar. But it was already too dark in the street to make
out his features.

Heurtin watched the receding trio for a moment or two, then turned and slouched off himself, followed by Lucas.

Maigret went back toward the bar.

"Police Judiciaire!" he said to the manager. "Who is he?"

"I think Radek's the name. He has his letters addressed here. He's a Czech."

"What's he do?"

"Nothing," answered the barman. "Sits there just as you saw him, dreaming. Sometimes he writes."

"Do you know where he lives?"

"No."

"Has he got any friends?"

"I don't think I've ever seen him say a word to a soul."

Maigret paid his bill, went out, and jumped into a taxi.

"The local Commissariat, please."

When he got there, Radek was sitting on a bench awaiting his turn. There were four or five foreigners there who had come to register with the police.

Maigret went straight through to where the district inspector was dealing with a young woman who, in three or four central European languages, was trying to tell him of the theft of some jewelry.

"Hallo! Are you working in this neighborhood?" asked the district inspector, surprised.

"Finish with the lady first."

"I can't understand a word of it. She's been telling me the same thing over and over again for the last half hour."

Maigret did not even smile, while the woman, getting

more and more incensed, began her story for the twentieth
time, pointing to her ringless fingers.

When at last she was got rid of, Maigret said:

"A man called Radek or something like that is being
brought up before you. I'll be here. Let him pass the night
in the cells and then release him."

"What's he done?"

"Eaten caviar and then couldn't pay."

"At the Dôme?"

"No, at the Coupole."

A bell was rung.

"Bring in Radek."

He strolled in as cool as could be, his hands in his pockets, and stood waiting in front of the two men, meeting
their stare unflinchingly, while a delighted smile played
around his lips.

"You know what you're charged with?"

Radek nodded. He wanted to light another cigarette,
but it was snatched out of his hands.

"What have you got to say?"

"Nothing at all."

"Where do you live? Have you any means of support?"

Radek produced a shabby passport, which he laid on
the desk.

"You know you're liable to fifteen days?"

"But the sentence would be suspended," corrected the
accused quietly. "You'd have to say it was a first offense."

"This says you're a medical student. Is that right?"

"Professor Grollet, whose name you have no doubt heard, will tell you that I was his best pupil."

And turning to Maigret he said with a touch of irony in his voice:

"I suppose, monsieur, that you're a policeman too?"

# 6

## CAVIAR AGAIN

Madame Maigret sighed but said nothing as her husband went out at seven in the morning after gulping down a cup of coffee, apparently quite unaware that it was scalding hot.

He had been absorbed and uncommunicative when he came home long after midnight, and now, as he left, he had an obstinate look on his face.

As he stalked through the corridors of the Préfecture he could not help noticing the way his colleagues looked at him, his subordinates, and even the messengers—a look of curiosity mixed with a certain admiration, and perhaps a shade of pity.

But he shook hands as though nothing was the matter, just as he had kissed his wife's forehead on leaving. Getting to his room, he poked up the fire and spread out his wet overcoat over a couple of chairs.

*"Le commissariat du quartier Montparnasse!"* he called in a leisurely voice into the telephone.

He puffed away at his pipe and began to sort out the papers on his desk.

"Hallo! Who's that? The duty sergeant? Inspector Maigret speaking of the P.J. You've released Radek? What's that? An hour ago? And you're sure our man, Janvier, was waiting for him? . . . Hallo! Yes . . . He didn't sleep, you say? . . . And smoked all his fags? Thanks, no, don't bother . . . If I want to know anything further I'll call around."

He took the Czech's passport from his pocket, a little grayish book bearing the arms of Czechoslovakia, nearly every page of which was covered with visas and the stamps of frontier officials.

Johann Radek, twenty-five years of age, born at Brno of unknown father. From the rubber stamps it could be seen that he had resided in Berlin, Mainz, Bonn, Turin, and Hamburg.

He was stated to be a medical student. As for his mother, Elizabeth Radek, deceased two years previously, she had been in employment as a domestic servant.

"What are your means of subsistence, young man?" Maigret had asked the evening before in the Commissariat de Police of Montparnasse.

And the prisoner, with a disdainful smile, had answered:

"Am I to call you 'young man' too?"

"Answer!"

"As long as my mother was alive, she used to send me enough money for me to study medicine."

"Out of her wages as a servant?"

"Yes. I was her only son. She'd have gone through fire for me. Does that surprise you?"

"But she died two years ago. Since then . . . ?"

"Some distant relations sent me a little money from time to time . . . Then some Czechs here in Paris have helped me occasionally . . . And sometimes I've had some translating to do."

"And the editor of the *Sifflet*?"

"I'm afraid I don't understand."

He said that with such obvious sarcasm as to make it mean "You're doing fine, my good fellow, but you haven't got me yet!"

And Maigret had not pursued the subject further but had walked back to the Coupole, where there was now no trace of Joseph Heurtin or of Lucas. The wanderer had plunged back into Paris with the detective on his heels.

Maigret had hailed a taxi.

"Hôtel George V."

He entered just as William Kirby, in a dinner jacket, was standing at the office counter changing some hundred-dollar notes.

"Do you want me?" he asked, seeing the inspector.

"Not unless you know a man called Radek."

People were coming and going in the Louis XVI entrance hall. The hotel employee was dealing out hundred-franc notes in pinned bundles of ten.

"Radek?"

Maigret looked the American straight in the eyes, but the latter seemed quite unconcerned.

"No. But you might ask Mrs. Kirby. She'll be down in

a moment. We're dining with some friends . . . There's a charity gala at the Ritz."

As he spoke, Mrs. Kirby came out of the lift with a shiver, hugging her ermine cape. She looked at the police officer with some astonishment.

"What is it?"

"Nothing to worry about. I'm looking for a man called Radek."

"Radek? Does he live here?"

Kirby pocketed his money and held out his hand to Maigret.

"You'll excuse us, won't you? We're late already."

The car that had been waiting for them glided off over the asphalt.

———

The telephone rang.

"Hallo! Inspector Maigret? Monsieur Coméliau would like to speak to you."

"Tell him I'm not in yet. Understand?"

At that time of the morning the examining magistrate must be ringing up from home. No doubt he was having his *petit déjeuner* in his dressing gown, feverishly turning over the pages of his newspaper, his mouth as usual twitching nervously.

"Hallo! Jean! Have there been any other calls for me? Did Coméliau leave any message?"

"Will you ring him up as soon as you get here. He'll be

at home till nine, and then in his office. Hallo! Wait a moment. Here's a call coming through now. Hallo! Hallo! Inspector Maigret? Yes, Monsieur Janvier, I'll put you through."

And a moment later Maigret heard:

"Is that you, inspector?"

"He's got away, what?"

"Yes, he has. I can't understand it at all. I was only twenty paces from him."

"What happened? Quick!"

"I can't think how it happened, because I'm certain he hadn't seen me."

"Go on."

"First, he walked about the place. Then he went into the Gare Montparnasse. Just when the suburban trains were coming in thick and fast. So I got close to him so's not to lose him in the crowd."

"But you lost him all the same."

"Not in the crowd. He got into a train that had just come in, without having any ticket. I stopped a second to ask a porter where the train went, without taking my eyes off it. And by the time I had got in he'd gone. Nipped out the other side, of course."

"Naturally!"

"What shall I do now?"

"Go and wait for me in the bar of the Coupole. Don't be surprised at anything . . . And above all, don't worry."

"I swear, inspector . . ."

Janvier was only twenty-five, and his voice sounded like that of a boy on the point of bursting into tears.

"That's all right. At the Coupole, then . . ."

Maigret hung up, then lifted the receiver again.

"Hôtel George V. Hallo! Yes. Is Mr. William Kirby there? No, don't disturb him. But what time did he get back last night? At three? With Mrs. Kirby? Thank you. Hallo! What do you say? He gave orders not to call him before eleven? Thanks. No, no message. I'll be seeing him myself."

The inspector filled his pipe and made sure the stove was stoked up to the top.

At that moment, to anyone who did not know him, he would have given the impression of a man sure of himself, making straight for an inevitable goal. He threw his head back and blew a cloud of smoke up to the ceiling. He joked with the messenger who brought in the morning papers.

But as soon as he was alone again he went back to the telephone.

"Hallo! Nothing from Lucas yet?"

"Nothing so far, inspector."

And Maigret bit hard on the mouthpiece of his pipe. It was now nine o'clock. Since five o'clock the previous afternoon! That was when Joseph Heurtin had disappeared around the corner of the Boulevard Raspail with Lucas following.

Was it conceivable that the latter had not had a chance,

in all those sixteen hours, either to telephone or to slip a
note into some policeman's hand?

Maigret was visibly anxious. He rang through to Dufour, who came to the telephone himself.

"Are you better?"

"Yes, I'm already on my feet again. Tomorrow I hope to
be able to come round to the Quai des Orfèvres for a bit . . .
But it's going to leave a hell of a scar. The doctor took the
dressing off yesterday and I had a look at it. It's a marvel
my head wasn't broken in two . . . Anyhow you've got
your man, I hope."

"Don't worry about that. Look here, I've got to ring off
now, as someone's trying to get through to me, and I'm
waiting for a call."

It was stifling in the room, with the stove roaring away
and the metal getting red-hot in places. Maigret was not
disappointed: it was Lucas telephoning.

"Hallo! Is that you, chief? Hallo! Don't cut me off,
mademoiselle. Police! Hallo!"

"I can hear you. Where are you?"

"At Morsang."

"Where's that?"

"A little village on the Seine, thirty-five kilometers from
Paris."

"And your friend?"

"He's safe. At his parents'."

"So you're close to Nandy?"

"Four kilometers off. I came here to telephone, so's not
to give the show away. What a night we've had!"

"Tell me all about it."

"First we wandered about the streets. All over the shop. He didn't seem to care where he went. At eight o'clock we stopped at a public soup kitchen in the Rue Réaumur, where he waited nearly two hours for his ration."

"So he'd no more money."

"Then he set off again. It's incredible how the Seine attracts him. We followed it, sometimes upstream, sometimes down. Hallo! Don't cut me off. Are you there?"

"Yes, go on."

"In the end we got toward Charenton, still keeping to the river. I expected him to look for a place to sleep under one of the bridges . . . You ought to have seen him! He could hardly stand. But no. We went right through Charenton and on to Alfortville, where he made for the road leading to Villeneuve-Saint-Georges. It was pitch-black and soaking wet. Cars splashing by every thirty seconds. If I had to begin that over again!"

"You will, my boy. But go on."

"That's all. Only there was thirty-five kilometers of it. You can't imagine what it was like. It was raining just about as hard as it could . . . Anyhow, he didn't notice anything. At Corbeil I nearly took a taxi to follow him with . . . At six this morning we were still on the go, one behind the other, crossing the wood between Morsang and Nandy."

"Did he go in at the door when he got home?"

"Do you know the place? Quite a humble roadside inn. They also sell newspapers and tobacco, and various oddments . . . No, he didn't go straight in, but skirted around

to the back by a narrow path and then jumped over a wall.
I saw him go into an outhouse, the sort of place where you
might keep a couple of goats."

"Nothing else?"

"Nothing much. Half an hour later his father came out
and opened the shutters. He appeared quite natural. I
went in and had a drink. Certainly he didn't seem to be in
the least upset. I managed to catch a gendarme cycling
along the road. I got him to puncture a tire and make that
a pretext for stopping at the inn until I got back."

"Good!"

"You think so? But then you're not splashed with mud
from head to foot. My socks are like sponges, and it's got
right through to my shirt . . . What shall I do?"

"You might change if you've got your luggage with you."

"If I'd had to carry a trunk too!"

"Well, get back to Nandy. Tell them anything you like:
that you're waiting for a friend who's asked you to meet
him there."

"Are you coming?"

"I can't tell. But, you know, if Heurtin gets away again,
it'll just about finish me off."

Maigret rang off and looked vacantly about him. Then
through a half-open door he called to his clerk:

"Look here! As soon as I've gone, ring up Monsieur
Coméliau and tell him . . . let me see . . . tell him all's going
well and that I'll keep him posted. You understand?
Nicely . . . with lots of polite phrases."

At eleven he got out of a taxi outside the Coupole. The first person he saw as he pushed his way through the door of the bar was Janvier, who, like all beginners, thought he was playing his part well by concealing three-quarters of his person behind a newspaper whose pages he never turned.

In the opposite corner, Johann Radek was carelessly stirring his *café-crème*.

He was freshly shaved, had on a clean shirt, and it even looked as though he had run a comb through his frizzy hair.

But the dominant impression he gave was one of intense interior jubilation.

The barman recognized Maigret and gave him a significant look, while Janvier behind his paper went through almost a pantomime of meaningful glances.

This subtle comedy, however, was rendered superfluous by Radek, who immediately addressed himself to Maigret:

"May I offer you something?"

He had half risen from his seat. He barely smiled, but there was not a feature of his face that did not betray a keen intelligence.

Maigret went forward, broad and heavy, seized a chair with a hand that could have crushed it, and lowered himself onto it.

"So you're back again?" he said, looking elsewhere.

"Yes. Those gentlemen were most considerate. It seems

that my case can't come up in less than a fortnight, so meanwhile they've let me go . . . But it's rather late for coffee. How would you like some vodka and some caviar sandwiches? . . . Barman!"

The barman blushed to the ears. He was visibly reluctant to serve this preposterous customer.

"I trust you won't ask me to pay in advance, considering that I'm in company," Radek went on.

And turning to Maigret, he explained:

"These people don't understand a thing. Would you believe it, when I came in just now they didn't want to serve me? He went straight off to fetch the manager without saying a word. And the manager asked me to go . . . I had to chuck some money on the table . . . Funny, isn't it?"

He said it all gravely, almost dreamily.

"Now, if I was a flashy young loafer like some of those gigolos you saw here yesterday, they'd give me as much credit as I wanted. But just because I'm a man of character . . . Yes, it's funny, isn't it? . . . You know, inspector, we must talk it over one of these days, us two. Perhaps you won't understand everything . . . All the same, I think you pride yourself on being an intelligent person . . ."

The waiter put the caviar sandwiches down on the table, not without a furtive glance at Maigret.

"Sixty francs."

Radek smiled. In the other corner, Janvier was still in ambush behind his paper.

"A packet of Abdullas," ordered the red-haired Czech.

And while they were being brought, he felt in one of the

side pockets of his jacket and ostentatiously produced a crumpled thousand-franc note, which he threw on the table.

"What were we saying, inspector? . . . But you'll excuse me. I've suddenly remembered I must ring up my tailor."

The telephones were in the large room next door, which had several exits. Maigret did not budge. But Janvier got up automatically and followed at a discreet distance.

They came back a few minutes later, one behind the other, and Janvier gave an affirmative nod to his chief. Radek really had telephoned a tailor.

# 7

# A FAMILY IN TROUBLE

"Let me give you some good advice, inspector."

Radek had lowered his voice to a confidential tone and was leaning over toward Maigret.

"Of course I know perfectly well what you'll be thinking. But, you see, it doesn't matter to me what you think, not the slightest . . . All the same, I'd like to give you a bit of advice. Leave it alone. Don't waste your time beating rotten eggs."

Maigret sat there stolidly, looking straight in front of him.

"You go on poking around, yet you haven't got the faintest idea . . ."

The Czech was warming up, though in a quiet, almost dull way that was characteristic of the man. Out of the corner of his eye, Maigret noticed his hands, long hands, astonishingly white and slightly freckled. They seemed to warm up to the subject too, and to take part in the conversation.

"Don't think for a moment that I'm throwing doubt on your professional capacity. If in this case you understand nothing—no, less than nothing—it's because right from the start you've been working on falsified data. And once on the wrong track, everything was inevitably wrong. Isn't that so? And all that you find out will be wrong, to the very end . . .

"On the other hand, the few things that might have helped you escaped your notice . . .

"For instance, you must admit that you failed to notice the part played all along by the Seine. The house at Saint-Cloud is on the banks of the Seine. The Rue Monsieur-le-Prince is five minutes' walk from the Seine. The Citanguette, where the papers say he hid after his escape—on the Seine too. Heurtin was born at Melun, on the banks of the Seine. His parents live at Nandy, on the banks of the Seine!"

The Czech's eyes were laughing, though the rest of his face was grave.

"You're quite at a loss to know what I'm up to, aren't you? It looks as though I was anxious to put my head in a noose. You don't ask me a single question, and here I am, plunging into the very subject in which you're dying to get me involved . . . But how can I be brought into it? I've nothing to do with Heurtin. I've nothing to do with Kirby. Nothing to do with Mrs. Henderson, nor with her maid . . . All you could bring up against me is that yesterday this Joseph Heurtin was wandering about outside, and that he seemed to be looking for me . . .

"Maybe he was. Maybe he wasn't . . . Anyhow, the fact remains that I left the place escorted by a couple of policemen . . .

"But does that prove anything . . . ?

"I tell you again you don't understand the first thing about it. And what's more, you never will . . .

"What am I doing in this business? Nothing at all. Or possibly everything!

"Just imagine an intelligent man—more than intelligent—who has nothing to do, who just spends his days sitting and thinking, and imagine that he has the opportunity to study a problem that touches on his own subject—for, after all, medicine and criminology overlap . . ."

Maigret's stubborn stillness was exasperating. He didn't even seem to be listening. The young man's voice rose a tone higher as he went on:

"Well, what do you say to it, inspector? Are you ready to admit that you're groping in the dark? No? Not yet? Well, allow me to tell you that you're making a big mistake, having got a conviction, to let your man go. You may never find anybody else to take his place. And there's always the possibility that he'll get away altogether . . .

"We were talking just now about false tracks. Shall I give you further proof? And shall I give you at the same time the pretext you need in order to arrest me?"

He swallowed down his vodka at a gulp and leaned back in his seat, thrusting a hand into one of the side pockets of his jacket.

When he brought it out, it was full of hundred-franc notes pinned together in bundles of ten. There were ten packets.

"You see? Brand-new notes. In other words, notes that

can easily be traced. Trace them! Have a good time! Unless, of course, you'd rather go home to bed, which is what I would really advise . . ."

He got up. Maigret remained sitting, looking him over from head to foot and blowing out a thick cloud of smoke from his pipe.

Customers were beginning to arrive.

"Would you like to arrest me?"

Maigret was in no hurry to answer. He took up the notes, contemplating them before putting them in his pocket.

At last he too got up, though so slowly that Radek could not help wincing. Gently he put two fingers on the young man's shoulder.

It was the old Maigret once more. Powerful, placid, sure of himself.

"Listen, sonny."

It was in such complete contrast to the pitch of Radek's voice, his nervous figure, his keen eyes, sparkling with another sort of intelligence altogether.

Maigret was by twenty years the elder, and the difference could be felt.

"Listen, sonny."

Janvier, as he overheard the words, could hardly keep from laughing, so delighted was he to see his chief once more at the top of his form.

And the latter merely added with the same casual good humor:

"We'll meet again one of these days, don't you worry."

Whereupon he nodded to the barman, stuffed his hands in his coat pockets, and went out.

———————

"As far as I can tell, they're the ones," said the man in the Hôtel George V, examining the bundles of banknotes that Maigret had handed him. "But there was much more than that. There was ten thousand in hundred-franc notes, the rest in thousands. A hundred thousand francs altogether."

A few moments later he had rung through to the bank.

"Hallo! Have you got the numbers of the notes I sent for yesterday? Not the thousands—only the hundreds."

He jotted down the numbers with a pencil, rang off, and turned to the inspector.

"Yes, they're the ones. I hope there's not going to be any trouble?"

"Not the slightest . . . Are Mr. and Mrs. Kirby in?"

"They went out half an hour ago."

"You saw them yourself?"

"As clearly as I see you."

"Are there many exits?"

"Two, but the other's only used by the staff."

"You told me Mr. and Mrs. Kirby got back at three o'clock this morning. Since then, has anybody been to see them?"

Maids, porters, and lift boys were asked in turn. And there seemed no doubt whatever that between three o'clock and eleven the Kirbys had not left their rooms, nor had they received any visitors.

"Have they sent anybody out with a letter?"

No. That too seemed out of the question.

From the previous afternoon up till seven that morning Radek had been in custody. He could not have communicated with anyone during that time. At seven he had been released with hardly any money in his pockets. Toward eight he had given Janvier the slip at the Gare Montparnasse.

And then at ten o'clock he was back at the Coupole with at least eleven thousand francs in his possession, of which ten thousand at any rate had incontestably been in William Kirby's pocket the evening before.

"Do you mind if I go upstairs and have a look around?"

It was referred to the manager. He didn't like the idea, but couldn't very well say no. The lift took Maigret up to the third floor.

It was the typical suite of a palatial hotel. Two bedrooms, two bathrooms, two sitting rooms. The beds were still unmade, the breakfast trays still there. In one bedroom a valet was brushing Kirby's dress clothes, while in the other his wife's evening dress was thrown over the back of a chair. Various objects were lying about: cigarette cases, a lady's handbag, a walking stick, a novel.

Back in the street, Maigret took a taxi and drove around to the Ritz where he was assured that the Kirbys with Miss Edna Reichberg had sat at table No. 18 the night before. They had arrived about nine and had not left till after half past two. No, the maître d'hôtel had noticed nothing unusual.

"But those notes! . . ." groaned Maigret as he crossed the Place Vendôme.

He stopped suddenly and was nearly caught by the wing of a limousine.

"Why the devil should Radek have shown them to me? Worse still—they're in my pocket now, and I should be hard-pressed to find a legal reason for their being there . . . And then that story of the Seine . . ."

On a sudden impulse he stopped a taxi.

"How long will it take you to drive to Nandy? It's a bit further than Corbeil."

"An hour, with the roads so slippery."

"Right. And stop at the first tobacconist's."

And Maigret spent an hour after his own heart, snugly ensconced in a corner of the cab, whose windows were splashed with rain and misty from the warmth inside. He smoked incessantly, warmly wrapped in the enormous overcoat that had become a byword on the Quai des Orfèvres.

The suburbs of Paris glided by, then the October country. Sometimes a drab band of river came into view between the gables of houses and the bare trees.

"Radek could only have one motive in talking to me like that and showing me those notes," thought Maigret. "He wants to sidetrack me by dragging a red herring across the trail . . .

"But why? To give Heurtin time to escape? To compromise Kirby? . . .

"But at the same time he's compromising himself."

The Czech's words came back to him:

"Right from the start you've been working on falsified data."

*Parbleu!* Wasn't that exactly what Maigret thought? Wasn't that why he had got the case reopened, although a verdict had been pronounced?

But to what extent had it been falsified? And how? After all, the material evidence against Heurtin was formidable. It couldn't all have been faked.

Admittedly Heurtin's shoes could have been borrowed by the murderer, but not his fingerprints, which had been found all over the place, even on the sheets and the curtains. How could they have been faked?

Then Heurtin had unquestionably been seen at midnight at the Pavillon Bleu. And he had got back to the Rue Monsieur-le-Prince at four.

"You don't understand the first thing about it. And, what's more, you never will." That's what Radek had said, this Czech who had suddenly sailed into the middle of the picture, though a moment before his very existence had been unknown.

The previous day at the Coupole, William Kirby had not so much as glanced at Radek. And when Maigret had pronounced the name at the hotel he had not seen the faintest glint of recognition come into the American's eyes.

Yet that didn't alter the fact that several bundles of hundred-franc notes had passed out of his pocket into the other's.

And to crown it all, it was Radek himself who seemed

anxious that the police should know. More than that even—
was he not positively clamoring for the principal part in
the play?

"Between the time Janvier lost him at the Gare Montparnasse and the time I found him at the Coupole he had
changed his shirt and had a shave. And it was during that
time that he came into possession of the money . . .

"Anyhow, he could hardly have had time to get to
Nandy and back," said Maigret to himself, trying to derive
some consolation from that conclusion.

The village was on the plateau that looks down on the
valley of the Seine. The west wind swept across it in gusts,
bending the trees. Ploughed fields stretched as far as the
eye could see. In the distance, a man with a gun looked
tiny in that great expanse.

"Where shall I take you?" asked the driver, opening the
window behind him.

"To the entrance of the village . . . And wait for me."

It was just one long street, in the middle of which was
the inn. Its sign bore the name: Evariste Heurtin.

A bell rang as Maigret pushed open the door and entered a room hung with oleographs. There was no one
there, though Lucas's hat was hanging on a nail.

"Hallo! Anyone there?" called Maigret.

He heard steps over his head, but it was a good five
minutes before anyone came down. It was a man in his six-
ties, fairly tall. There was an unnatural fixity in his blank
stare.

"What can I get you?" he asked, without coming through the doorway. Then almost at once he added:

"Do you belong to the police too?"

His voice was absolutely flat, his words hardly articulated. He said no more, but merely pointed to the staircase at the foot of which he was standing. Then slowly he went upstairs again.

The stairs were narrow, the walls whitewashed. From above came confused sounds. When one of the bedroom doors was opened, the first thing Maigret saw was Lucas standing by the window. He was looking down and didn't see the inspector for a moment.

Then a bed with a figure bending over it. And an old woman hunched up in an old-fashioned armchair.

The room was large, the beams showing in the ceiling, the wallpaper peeling off here and there. The deal floor creaked at every footfall.

"Shut that door," said the man bending over the bed, peremptorily.

It was a doctor. His bag was lying open on the round mahogany table. At last Lucas, looking thoroughly disconcerted, came up to Maigret.

"Here already?" he asked. "I hardly expected you so soon."

It was Joseph Heurtin lying on the bed, his chest bare, skin livid, ribs sticking out. He looked like some broken object.

The old woman was whining and groaning. The father

went and stood by the head of the bed. His stare was actually frightening, it was so utterly expressionless.

"Come outside," said Lucas, "and I'll tell you what's happened."

They went out. On the landing Lucas hesitated, then opened the door of another bedroom, and the two went in. The room had not yet been done, and women's clothes were lying about. The window looked out on to the yard behind the house where the hens were paddling about in the soaking manure.

"Well?"

"A rotten morning, I assure you. As soon as I'd telephoned I came back here, making a sign to the gendarme that he was no longer wanted. I sat in the room downstairs trying to guess what was going on in the house.

"The old man was in the room with me. He asked if I wanted anything to eat. I thought he looked at me a bit suspiciously, particularly when I said I might be staying the night, as I was waiting for someone to meet me here.

"Some whispering began in the kitchen, and I saw the man was trying to listen. He looked a bit surprised, then called out: 'Is that you, Victorine?'

"There was no further sound for two or three minutes. Then his wife appeared, looking very strange, like someone who's thoroughly upset but wants to look natural.

"'I'm going for the milk,' she said.

"'But it's not yet time,' he answered.

"She went out all the same, just as she was, in her

sabots and a shawl over her head. As soon as she'd gone, old Heurtin went into the kitchen, where his daughter was.

"I could hear them talking and then the girl sobbing, but I only caught the words of one remark: 'I might have known it from the way your mother looked.'

"He strode out into the yard and I heard him open a door—no doubt the door of the outhouse where Joseph was hiding. It was an hour before he reappeared. Meanwhile the girl was serving drinks to some drivers. Her eyes were red and she couldn't look anybody in the face.

"The mother had come back and there had been more whisperings behind the scenes. When old Heurtin reappeared he looked just as you saw him.

"It was only afterward that I understood all these comings and goings . . . The women had discovered Joseph in the outhouse and had decided to tell the old man nothing about it. He, however, realized that there was something up. When his wife went out he pumped the girl, who couldn't keep the secret. As soon as he knew, he went out to the outhouse and told Joseph to clear out.

"You noticed him, I expect . . . A very decent sort, and no doubt pretty strict in his ideas of right and wrong . . . At the same time he guessed who I was . . .

"I don't think he'd have handed his boy over to me. In fact, I dare say he was ready to help him get away. But he wouldn't let him stay.

"Anyhow, about ten o'clock I was standing at the window looking out onto the yard, and I saw Madame

Heurtin sneaking along in her stockings in spite of the rain, making for the outhouse.

"A few seconds later she was screaming for help . . . It was a nasty sight, I can tell you . . . I got there at the same moment as the old man, and I swear I saw the sweat fairly spurt out on his temples.

"The fellow was in such a strange position against the wall. In fact, you had to get quite close to see that he'd hanged himself on a nail.

"Old Heurtin had more presence of mind than me. It was he who cut him down. He stretched the boy out on the straw and got his tongue forward, at the same time shouting to his daughter to go for a doctor.

"The whole household was of course in a fearful state. Well, you've seen for yourself how things are. It's quite upset me too.

"But apart from the family and the doctor, no one knows anything. In the village they think it's Madame Heurtin that's ill . . . His father and I carried him upstairs together. The doctor's been at him for the best part of an hour. It seems there's a good chance of bringing him around . . . The old man hasn't spoken a word the whole time. On the other hand, the girl got hysterical and they shut her up in the kitchen so that she wouldn't be heard from the street."

A door opened, and Maigret, going out onto the landing, caught the doctor just about to leave. They went down together, and Maigret drew the other aside.

"Police Judiciaire, doctor. How is he?"

It was a country doctor, who was at no pains to hide his lack of sympathy for the police.

"Are you going to take him away?" he asked, somewhat disagreeably.

"I don't know. It depends on how he is."

"They found him just in time. But it will take him some days to recover. I suppose it's at the Santé that he got in this pitiable condition. One might think there was not a drop of blood in his veins."

"I must ask you not to speak of this to anyone . . ."

"The request is unnecessary. We have a code in our profession."

Joseph's father had followed them down. His eyes were fixed on Maigret, but he didn't ask any questions. Mechanically he took the two empty glasses that were standing on the bar and rinsed them in the sink.

A minute went by. A bad minute, hardly bearable. The three men could hear the sound of sobbing coming from the kitchen. Maigret sighed.

"Would you like to keep him here a few days?" he asked, looking at the old man.

No answer.

"I should have to leave one of my men in the house . . ."

The innkeeper's eyes were turned for a moment on Lucas, who had now joined them. Then he looked down again at the glasses he was drying. A tear ran down his cheek.

"He swore to his mother . . ." he began. But he turned his head away, unable to go on. To recover his composure he poured himself out a glass of rum, though it seemed to cost him an effort to swallow it down.

Maigret, turning to Lucas, merely grunted:

"Stay here."

He did not leave the place at once, but went along the passage and out into the yard. Through the kitchen window he could see the girl leaning against the wall, her head buried in her arms.

On the other side of the manure heap the door of the outhouse was wide open. A bit of cord still hung from a stout iron nail.

The inspector retraced his steps, finding only Lucas in the café.

"Where's he gone?"

"Upstairs."

"He said nothing, I suppose? I'll send somebody to take turns with you. Ring me up twice a day."

"It's you who did it, I tell you. It's you who killed him," cried out the old woman upstairs between her tears. "Go away. You've killed him . . . My boy . . . My own little boy! . . ."

A bell rang. It was Maigret opening the door. He walked off to find his taxi on the outskirts of the village.

# 8

# A MAN IN THE HOUSE

Maigret got out of a taxi in front of the Hendersons' house at Saint-Cloud. It was just after three. After getting back from Nandy, he had remembered that he had never returned the key given him in July when he was making his investigations.

He went there without any precise motive. There was just a chance that he might stumble on some clue that he had so far overlooked. Or perhaps the mere atmosphere of the place might give him an idea.

The house was a substantial though ugly building, flanked by a turret and surrounded by a good-sized rambling garden. The shutters were closed. The garden paths were littered with dead leaves.

Maigret opened the gate and approached the house. He could not help being oppressed by the desolate look of it all. It was more like a cemetery than a place for living people.

Almost reluctantly, he went up the four steps, on either side of which were pretentious plaster figures. A lantern of wrought iron overhung the door. Inside, it took him a moment or two to get used to the semidarkness of the hall.

There was something sordid about this mixture of luxury and decay. The ground floor had not been used for four years, that is to say, ever since Mr. Henderson's death. Yet most of the furniture, and even ornaments, had been left just as they were.

When Maigret went into the drawing room, the cut-glass chandelier tinkled in the draft. The parquet floor creaked under his tread.

He switched on the light to see if it was working. A dozen lamps out of twenty instantly went on, but so thick was the dust on them that they glowed only dimly.

Valuable rugs had been rolled up and stacked in one corner. The armchairs had all been pushed against the wall. A few trunks were lying about. One was empty, while another, smelling strongly of mothball, contained some of the dead man's clothes. And it was four years since he'd died.

The place had glittered in his day. In that very room grand receptions had been given, and the names of the guests had been reported in the papers. On the huge mantelpiece was a half-consumed box of cigars.

The story of its former occupants was written in that room. The past lay there heavy and oppressive.

A couple that had no doubt been happy, that had at any rate led a brilliant social life, with friends in most of the capitals of Europe. Then Mrs. Henderson, widowed at seventy, too tired to carry on that life alone. Too tired even to move to a smaller house, she had simply shut herself up in her own suite of rooms upstairs, leaving the rest of the house to take care of itself.

Nothing was left of all the brilliance but a sequestered old lady with her maid-companion . . .

And then one night she was . . .

Maigret wandered on through two other reception rooms and then through a handsomely furnished dining room. Leaving that, he found himself back in the hall at the foot of the stairs, which were of marble up to the first floor.

The slightest noise resounded in the empty house.

The Kirbys had not touched anything. It was doubtful whether they had even set foot in the place since their aunt's death. A house utterly abandoned. So much so that Maigret found on one of the stairs a candle that he had used during his investigations in July.

On the first-floor landing he stopped suddenly, gripped by an uneasy feeling that he could not analyze for a moment. When he did, he held his breath and listened.

Hadn't he heard something? No, he couldn't be sure. But somehow or other he had most definitely the impression that he was not alone. Obscurely he had sensed a flicker of life in that empty house.

He shrugged his shoulders, however, and went on. But on opening the door in front of him he frowned and sniffed.

Yes, that was the smell of tobacco smoke. And not stale either. Somebody had been smoking there very recently.

He walked on rapidly and found himself in the dead woman's boudoir. The door to the bedroom was ajar. Pushing it open, Maigret saw nobody, but the smell was more unmistakable than ever. And there on the floor was some fine cigarette ash, clearly visible even in that dim light.

"Who's there?"

He would have liked to have been calmer, but he could not help an uneasy feeling.

After all, wasn't the whole setting enough to be disturbing? In the bedroom signs of the carnage were hardly obliterated. One of Mrs. Henderson's dresses was still there just as it had been flung over the back of a chair. The light came in strips between the slats of the shutters. And in that dim interior someone was moving.

For this time it was definitely audible: a metallic noise coming from the bathroom.

Maigret strode forward, but when he got there it was empty. He could now hear steps quite clearly on the other side of a door leading to a lobby.

Automatically he felt for his revolver. He rushed through that door too, and on the other side of the lobby saw the back stairs. It was light here, as the staircase windows had no shutters.

Someone was going upstairs, and obviously trying to do so as quietly as possible. Maigret called out once more:

"Who's there?"

He was now thoroughly excited. Now, when he had really least expected it, the truth was perhaps falling into his hands.

He started running. A door slammed on the floor above. The fugitive hurried across a room, and another door opened and shut.

Maigret was gaining ground. As on the ground floor,

the rooms here, spare bedrooms, had been abandoned. Furniture and objects of all sorts were scattered about.

A vase crashed to the floor. The inspector feared one thing: that he'd come to a door that the other had had the presence of mind to lock behind him.

"In the name of the law! . . ." he shouted.

But the fugitive did not stop. They'd gone half around the second floor when his hand reached a doorknob at the same time as another on the other side felt for the key.

"Open, or . . ."

The key had turned. Almost without thinking what he was about, the inspector took three steps backward and hurled himself with all his weight against the large upper panel of the door.

The framework of the door was stout enough, but the panel was thin, and it creaked hopefully. In the other room a window was opened.

"In the name of the law! . . ." shouted Maigret again, oblivious of the fact that his presence in that house that now belonged to William Kirby was anything but legal, for he had no search warrant.

Twice, three times, his shoulder came against the panel, that was now beginning to crack. He was just mustering his strength for a fourth dive at it, when a shot rang out, followed by a silence so complete that Maigret remained standing in suspense, his lips parted.

"Who is it? Open that door!"

Not a sound. Not even a groan. Nor that characteristic clatter of a revolver falling.

Then with a burst of fury Maigret flung himself once more against the panel, which now gave way. Quickly he put his hand through the opening and unlocked the door.

A gust of cold damp air blew in at the open window, through which could be seen the lighted windows of a restaurant opposite and the yellow mass of a tram.

On the floor a man was sitting with his back to the wall, his body leaning slightly over to the left. The gray suit alone told Maigret it was William Kirby. It would have been difficult for anybody to identify the face, or what little was left of it.

The American must have put his revolver to the roof of his mouth, for half the head was blown away.

———

Once more Maigret wandered through the rooms. He walked slowly and gloomily, trying the switches at each door as he went through. Some of the lamps had no bulbs, but most had, so that before long the house was pretty well lit from top to bottom.

In Mrs. Henderson's bedroom he caught sight of a telephone by the bed. He lifted the receiver, just in case it had not been disconnected. An answering click told him it was still working.

Never had he had so strongly the impression of being in a house of death. There he was, sitting on the edge of the very bed in which the old lady had been stabbed, looking through the doorway across which Élise Chatrier's body had been found lying.

And there on the floor above was now a fresh corpse, sitting under an open window that let in the damp, chill, October air.

"Hallo! The Préfecture, please." In spite of himself, his voice was subdued.

"Hallo! Give me the Director of the P.J. Maigret speaking. Is that you, chief? . . . William Kirby has just shot himself in the Hendersons' house at Saint-Cloud . . . Hallo! Yes . . . I'm on the spot. Will you give orders for . . . Yes, I was here at the time. Only three or four yards away, but there was a door between us . . . Yes, I know . . . No, I can't explain anything. Later perhaps . . ."

After ringing off, he sat there for several minutes without moving, staring straight in front of him. Then he absentmindedly filled his pipe, but forgot to light it.

The house seemed to him like a huge, cold, empty box in which he was an infinitely small particle.

"Falsified data . . ." he muttered softly.

He thought of going upstairs again. But what was the use? The American was dead all right . . . His right hand still gripped the revolver with which he had shot himself.

Maigret snorted. He was thinking of Coméliau. He'd have heard about it by now. Most likely he'd be the one to come with the police experts of the Identité Judiciaire.

On the wall hung a life-size portrait in oils of Mr. Henderson, looking very solemn in evening dress with the Grand Cordon of the Légion d'Honneur and other decorations.

The inspector started wandering about again. He went into Élise Chatrier's room and opened a cupboard. Several dresses, some of silk, some of wool, were neatly hanging in a row.

His ear caught every sound outside, and he gave a sigh of relief when at last he heard two cars stop almost at the same moment outside the gate. There were voices in the garden. Monsieur Coméliau was saying in his most peevish tones:

"Really! It's inconceivable . . . Quite inconceivable . . ."

Maigret went downstairs like a host going down to receive his guests. When he opened the door, however, he merely said:

"This way."

He never forgot how the examining magistrate looked at him. Such a look! And the little man's lips really trembled with indignation before blurting out:

"I'm waiting for your explanation, inspector."

But Maigret simply led the way up to the room on the second floor, where he finally said:

"There you are."

"Did you ask him to meet you here?"

"No, I had no idea he was in the house . . . I came merely on the off chance of finding out something that might be useful."

"Where was he?"

"I suppose in his aunt's room. But he made off when I came up . . . I followed . . . He got this far, and then, as I was trying to break down the door, he shot himself."

By the look on Monsieur Coméliau's face you might

have thought he doubted Maigret's story. But really it only expressed his abiding horror of complications of any kind.

The doctor examined the body. Cameras were brought upstairs and photographs taken.

"Heurtin?" snapped Monsieur Coméliau.

". . . will take his place in the Santé whenever you like."

"So you've found him?"

Maigret shrugged his shoulders.

"Then the sooner he's locked up, the better."

"Just as you like, *Monsieur le Juge.*"

"Is that all you have to say to me?"

"All for the moment."

"You still think that . . . ?"

"That Heurtin's innocent? I've really nothing to tell you. I asked for ten days, and I haven't yet had two."

"Where are you going to now?"

"I don't know."

Maigret stuck his hands in his overcoat pockets and stood for a while watching the experts on the job. Then he turned and went downstairs again to Mrs. Henderson's room and picked up the telephone receiver.

"Hallo! Hôtel George V . . . Hallo! Will you tell me if Mrs. Kirby is there? . . . What's that? . . . Having tea? Thank you . . . No, no message."

Monsieur Coméliau had followed him down and was standing by the door looking at him sourly.

"You see what a mess you've made."

Without answering, Maigret put on his hat, saluted the

magistrate curtly, and went out. He had not kept his taxi, and had to walk right to the Saint-Cloud bridge before finding one.

———

Muted music. Couples dancing languidly. Pretty women, mostly foreigners, grouped around the tables of the elegant *salon de thé* of the Hôtel George V.

Maigret, who had with ill grace relinquished his overcoat to the cloakroom attendant, made for a group in which he had recognized Edna Reichberg and Mrs. Kirby.

They were listening to a young Scandinavian, who appeared to be telling some amusing story, for they were laughing continuously.

"Madame Kirby . . ." said the inspector with a bow.

She looked up at him with curiosity, then looked round at the other two, like someone who does not care to be disturbed.

"Yes, what is it?"

"Could you give me a few minutes?"

"Just now? Is it so urgent?"

But he was so grave that she got up without more ado and looked about her for a quiet corner.

"Come to the bar," she said. "No one goes there at this time of day."

The bar was empty. The two remained standing.

"Did you know your husband was going to Saint-Cloud this afternoon?"

"I don't understand. He's free to go wherever . . ."

"I'm asking you whether he spoke of going to the Hendersons' house."

"No."

"Have you been there together since the . . . ?"

She shook her head.

"Never. It's too melancholy."

"Your husband went there today, alone."

She began to be anxious, looking inquiringly into Maigret's eyes.

"Well?"

"He's had an accident."

"With his car? I always knew . . ."

Edna looked into the bar inquisitively on the pretext of searching for a handbag she had left somewhere.

"No, madame . . . Your husband tried to take his own life."

The young woman's eyes filled with astonishment, then with doubt. For an instant she seemed on the point of bursting into laughter.

"William?"

"He fired a revolver bullet into . . ."

Two feverish hands suddenly seized Maigret's wrists, while his ears were assailed by a flood of questions in English. Then suddenly she shuddered, let go of him, and drew back a step.

"It is my duty, madame, to tell you that your husband died two hours ago in the house at Saint-Cloud."

But Mrs. Kirby was no longer listening. She marched with long strides across the *salon de thé,* without a glance at Edna or the Scandinavian, went into the hall, and, bare-headed and empty-handed as she was, rushed out into the street.

The porter asked her:

"A taxi?"

But she was already getting into one, calling out:

"To Saint-Cloud . . . As quick as you can."

Maigret saw no point in following her. He collected his precious overcoat, and when a bus passed, going toward the Cité, he jumped onto the rear platform.

"Any calls for me?" he asked when he got to his office.

"One at two o'clock. There's a note on your desk."

The note was a message from Janvier.

"Tried on a suit at the tailor's. Lunch in a restaurant in the Boulevard Montparnasse. At two o'clock coffee at the Coupole. Has telephoned twice."

And since two? Maigret wondered, as he sank into his armchair, having previously locked his door. When he suddenly woke up, he was astonished to find it was half past ten.

"Has anyone telephoned?"

"Were you there? I thought you'd gone out. Monsieur Coméliau rang up twice."

"And Janvier?"

"No."

Half an hour later Maigret walked into the bar of the Coupole, where there was no sign of either Radek or Janvier. He drew the barman aside.

"Has the Czech been in again?"

"He spent the afternoon here with your friend . . . You know: the young man in the mackintosh."

"At the same table?"

"In this very corner. And they drank at least four whiskeys each."

"When did they go?"

"First of all they had dinner in the next room."

"Together?"

"Together . . . They left only a little while ago."

"You don't know where they went?"

"You might ask the boy outside. He got them a taxi."

The boy remembered.

"It was the blue one that's always standing opposite. They can't have gone very far, for there it is back again already."

A moment later the driver was saying:

"Yes, that's right. I took them to the Pélican in the Rue des Écoles."

"Well, take me there too, will you?"

Maigret stalked into the Pélican, looking anything but agreeable. He snubbed the page boy and then the waiter who wanted to take him into the *grande salle*.

He made straight for the bar, and there, among a throng of merrymakers and doubtful women, he found the two men he was looking for, perched on high stools in a corner.

At a glance he took in Janvier's sparkling eyes and highly colored cheeks. Radek, on the other hand, was staring at his glass in somber contemplation.

Maigret walked straight toward them, while Janvier, obviously the worse for liquor, made him signs that were intended to convey:

"Everything's all right . . . Just leave it to me . . . Don't let him see you . . ."

But Maigret came and stood right in front of them. Radek muttered rather thickly:

"Hallo! You here again?"

Janvier went on making signs, signs that he considered both very discreet and very expressive.

"Have a drink, inspector."

"Look here, Radek!"

"Barman, the same for monsieur."

And the Czech gulped down the mixture in his glass before saying:

"I'm listening . . . And you, Janvier, are you listening too?" And he gave Janvier a poke in the ribs.

"Is it long since you've been to Saint-Cloud?" asked Maigret slowly.

"Me? Ha! Ha! Ha! What a joke!"

"You know there's another corpse now?"

"A good job for the undertakers. Your health, inspector."

He wasn't acting. He was drunk. Not as drunk as Janvier, but enough for his eyes to be popping out of his head and for him to have to hold on to the rail around the bar to keep his balance.

"And who's the lucky fellow?"

"William Kirby."

For a few seconds Radek seemed to be battling with his intoxication, as though trying hard to appreciate the gravity of the news. Then he threw back his head with a laugh, making a sign to the barman to fill up the glasses.

"All right. So much the worse for you, old man."

"Meaning by that?"

"That you'll never understand. Less than ever . . . But didn't I tell you so at the start? . . . And now let me make a suggestion. We've already come to an understanding, Janvier and I. It's like this: you've taken it into your heads to follow me about. Good. It's all the same to me . . . Only, instead of marching foolishly one behind the other, taking cover in doorways, and all the rest, why shouldn't we all join together and have a good time? Wouldn't that be more intelligent? You see, we never know what the morrow may bring, so let's enjoy ourselves while we can . . . It's full of pretty girls here. We'll each choose one. Janvier's already made a pass at that little dark thing over there. For myself . . . well, I haven't quite made up my mind . . . And of course I do all the paying . . .

"Well, what do you say to it?"

He looked at the inspector, who looked back at him. And Maigret could no longer see the slightest sign of drunkenness on the young man's face.

Once more the pupils of those eyes were glittering with the keenest intelligence as they looked at him with superb derision. It was as though his whole being was in an ecstasy of triumph.

# 9

# THE NEXT DAY

It was eight in the morning. Maigret had parted with Radek and Janvier four hours earlier. He was now writing, slowly, with heavy black downstrokes, pausing after each paragraph to see what he had written and at the same time to take a sip at his black coffee.

July 7. Midnight. Heurtin drinks four grogs in quick succession at the Pavillon Bleu. Drops Rly. ticket.

July 8. About 2:00 a.m. The two women stabbed. Footprints and fingerprints are Heurtin's. 4:00 a.m. H. back in Rue Monsieur-le-Prince. He goes back to work as usual until arrested evening July 9. Denies murder, but was certainly at Saint-Cloud.

October 13. Plan of escape sent to Heurtin. He appears to have expected something of the sort.

Oct. 16. 2:00 a.m. Heurtin escapes, wanders about Paris, apparently without aim. Fetches up at Citanguette. Sleeps.

Morning papers report escape without comment. 10:00 a.m. Anonymous letter received at *Sifflet* saying escape was engineered by police. Moers examines letter.

Written at the Coupole in the American bar. Writing left-handed. Writer foreigner, linguist, intelligent. Coffee stain on paper. (Fits Radek.) Writer perhaps also subject to incurable disease.

6:00 p.m. Heurtin comes down. Dufour tries to take paper. Scuffle. Light smashed. H. gets away.

Oct. 17. About 1:00 p.m. Kirbys (just back from Biarritz) and Edna Reichberg in the American bar of the Coupole. Radek there eating yogurt. They do not seem to be acquainted.

Heurtin appears outside. Seems looking for someone. Kirbys go, but do not notice H. nor he them.

5:30 p.m. H. still waiting when only Radek left. R. then orders caviar, cigarettes, etc. Can't pay. Manager sends for police. R. marched off to commissariat, where he is detained. Heurtin, seeing Radek with police, makes off, followed by Lucas.

8:30 p.m. Hôtel G. V. William Kirby changing dollars into francs. Says he doesn't know Radek. Seems telling the truth. Goes off with Mrs. K. to Ritz. They are there at table No. 18 at 9:00 p.m. and stay till at least 2:30 a.m.

Heurtin wanders aimlessly about (has no more money), then makes for Nandy.

Oct. 18. About 6:30 a.m. H. gets to Nandy and hides in shed. Father finds him. Refuses to let him stay. H. tries to hang himself. Has been in bed since.

Paris. 7:00 a.m. Radek released. Shakes off Janvier
8:00 a.m. Gare Montparnasse. Enters Coupole bar
10:00 a.m. Shaved, clean shirt. Puts 1000-fr. note on table.

Yet the day before he had given himself out to be penniless and had certainly looked it.

A little later, when I come in, he offers me caviar and starts talking of the Henderson murder, though it has never been mentioned in his presence by the police.

He says the police will never understand the first thing about the case. Speaks of falsified data. Then throws down 10 bundles of 100-fr. notes, points out they can easily be traced, and practically challenges me to arrest him.

W. Kirby was back in Hôtel G. V. by 3:00 a.m. and does not leave again till 10:45. Yet Radek's notes are the ones Kirby got in his hotel when he changed his dollars.

Janvier stays at Coupole to keep track of R. Latter telephones twice.

3:00 p.m. Kirby is in the house at Saint-Cloud. He would hear me coming through the gate and up the path, would look through the shutters and recognize me. Retreats as I go upstairs. When cornered, shoots himself.

Mrs. Kirby is with Edna R. at Hôtel G. V. She seems to know nothing of his going to Saint-Cloud.

Radek and Janvier have dinner together and later go to Pélican, where I find them both pretty drunk.

Having got that far, Maigret stopped and sighed. What a night it had been! Radek had dragged them around from bar to bar, plying them with drinks and drinking freely himself. Sometimes he had seemed quite drunk, and then a minute later perfectly lucid. And all the time he had been throwing out hints, and telling Maigret the police were floundering.

At four o'clock he had got hold of a couple of girls, and had tried to persuade the others to follow his example. As they refused, he had gone off with his two ladies and taken a room in a hotel.

Since then Maigret had not seen him. But just before eight he had rung through to the hotel and been told:

"The two ladies are still in bed. Their friend has just paid the bill and left."

———

Maigret was feeling flat and stale to a degree he had very rarely known when on a job. He looked down with utter boredom at the notes he had been making. A colleague shook him by the hand, but he did not even say good morning, just making a sign that pleaded for him to be left in peace.

In the margin he wrote: "Find out what Kirby was doing between 10:45 and 3:00 p.m. yesterday."

Then suddenly, with a frown, he rang up the Coupole.

"I'd like to know how long it is since any letters came for Radek."

Five minutes later came the answer:

"At least ten days."

He put the same question to the little hotel where the Czech had a room.

"About a week."

Maigret next opened a directory and went through the list of the postes restantes in Paris. He finally selected the one in the Boulevard Raspail and rang up.

"Hallo! Poste Restante? Police Judiciaire speaking. Have you got a customer by the name of Radek? ... No? Well, he may use another name, or even initials ... Listen, mademoiselle, he's a foreigner, poorly dressed, red hair, long and frizzy ... You know him? Good ... Initials M. V.? ... And when did he last get a letter? ... Yes, find out, please. I'll wait. Don't ring off."

Someone knocked, and Maigret, without looking round, called out: "Come in," and went on talking.

"Hallo! Yes. What do you say? Yesterday morning at nine? It had come through the post, I suppose? Thank you. That's all—no, wait a moment. It was a bulky letter, wasn't it? ... Might have contained a packet of bank-notes? ..."

"Not so bad!" said a quiet voice just behind him.

The inspector turned around. It was Radek, looking thoroughly washed out, though there was just a suspicion of a twinkle in his eye. He sat down and went on:

"Of course it was childishly simple ... So you know now how I got the money. The evening before, it had been in the pocket of that poor fellow Kirby. But was it Kirby himself who posted it? That's what we'd like to know, isn't it?"

"How did you get here?"

"The man at the door was talking to somebody, and I just sailed in as if I belonged to the place. I wandered about a bit, and then saw your card on the door . . . Very clever, don't you think so? . . . And here we are, right in the bosom of the Police Judiciaire . . ."

Maigret scanned the tired face. Tired, certainly, but not so much from a sleepless night. There was something else. It was more like that of a sick man, a man who has just had some kind of attack. There were rings under his eyes. The lips were hardly red at all.

"Have you come to tell me something?"

"Nothing special. Thought I'd ask how you were getting on. You got back all right this morning?"

"Yes, thank you."

From where he sat, Radek could see the notes the inspector had been making, as much to while away the time as to help him get things straight in his mind. The shadow of a smile flitted across the young man's face.

"Do you remember the Taylor case?" he asked abruptly. "But I don't suppose you do, as you probably don't read the American papers . . . Well, Desmond Taylor, one of the best-known Hollywood film directors, was murdered in 1922. At least a dozen people's names were mentioned in connection with the case—film stars, beautiful women, etc. But no arrest was ever made.

"The case faded out. But there was an article about it not very long ago in an American magazine. Do you know what it said? I can remember every word of it. I've an excellent memory.

"It said: '*From the very beginning the police knew perfectly well who killed Desmond Taylor. But they had so lit-*

*tle evidence that, even if the murderer had given himself up, he would have had himself to undertake the prosecution. He would have had himself to furnish the evidence that would corroborate his confession.'"*

For a moment Maigret stared at the Czech with astonishment, while the latter, crossing his legs and lighting a cigarette, calmly went on:

"Yes . . . And it was the chief of police himself who said so. That's a year ago now . . . I remember every word of it . . . And of course Taylor's murderer is still in the best of health . . ."

The inspector had now relapsed into the casual indifference it was his role to assume. In the most classic manner he leaned back in his chair, put his feet up on his desk, and looked for all the world like a man who condescends to listen, but takes no great interest in the conversation.

"So you want to check up on the movements of William Kirby? . . . When the crime was committed the police never thought of that. Or perhaps they didn't dare!"

"Perhaps you can provide some information yourself?"

"Of course. But so could anybody in Montparnasse . . . First of all, at the time of his aunt's death he was up to his ears in debt. Six hundred thousand francs or more. Even Bob, the barman, had to lend him money . . ."

"It's often like that in these grand families . . . It was all very well being Henderson's nephew, but he had precious little himself. He'd another uncle with a colossal fortune, and a cousin who was chairman of one of the big American banks. But his father had been pretty well ruined ten years ago. So, you see, he was only a poor relation.

"And then all his uncles and aunts and cousins had children of their own. That is, all except the Hendersons. So his cue was obviously to hang about and wait for them to go. They were both in their seventies, so he wouldn't have to wait very long . . . What did you say?"

"Nothing."

Maigret's silence was visibly disconcerting to Radek, but he went on:

"You know as well as I do that if you've got the right kind of surname you can live without cash for a very long time . . . Besides, Kirby had the most winning ways . . . Never did a stroke of work, but all the more charming for that. Always good-humored. He loved life and loved everybody . . .

"Particularly women . . . And he was nice to them. Do anything for them . . . You saw him with his wife. He was very much in love with her . . .

"But that didn't stop him from . . . Fortunately there's a code among these people. So she never knew . . . I remember once: they were having a drink at the Coupole together. A girl who was hanging about caught his eye. Then he turned to Mrs. Kirby and said:

"'I'll be back in a moment. Just going to a shop around the corner.'

"And everybody in the place, save Mrs. Kirby, knew he was going to spend half an hour with that girl in the first hotel they came to in the Rue Delambre . . .

"It wasn't just once, nor even fifty times. And of course Edna Reichberg was his mistress too. Spending the whole day making up to her dear friend Mrs. Kirby, and then behind her back . . . Others too. Any amount of them . . .

"He could never say no to a woman. I really think he loved them all . . ."

Maigret yawned and stretched himself.

"Many a time when he'd barely a taxi fare in his pocket he'd stand two or three rounds, twelve or fifteen cocktails a time, to people he hardly knew by name . . . And how he used to laugh. I never saw him look worried . . . Just think of it: a being born under a happy star. Happy in his cradle, happy ever after. A person who loved everybody and was loved by everybody. A person in whom all is pardoned, even the most unpardonable things . . . Lucky too . . . I don't suppose you're a gambler. So you don't know what it feels like when the other chap cuts a seven and you promptly cut an eight. And in the next round when he cuts a king you go and cut an ace . . . Every time without fail. Not like us wretched human beings, but like the hero of a storybook. . . .

"Well, that hero's name was William Kirby . . .

"All the same, by the time Mrs. Henderson died he'd got pretty well to the end of his tether. In fact, I rather fancy he'd been reduced to imitating the signatures of some of his illustrious relations to keep his creditors quiet."

"He shot himself," said Maigret drily.

Radek laughed silently, a laugh impossible to fathom. He got up to throw his cigarette end into the coal scuttle, then came back to his place.

"Yes, he shot himself, but not *till yesterday*," he said enigmatically.

"Look here!"

Maigret's voice had suddenly got rough. He stood up and looked Radek hard in the eyes, then examined him from top to toe.

There was a moment's silence, almost nerve-racking, before Maigret went on:

"What the hell do you want with me?"

"I just dropped in for a chat . . . Or perhaps to do you a good turn. You must admit that it would have taken you quite a little time to collect the information I've given you in a few minutes . . . You might even like some more . . .

"Take that little Edna, for instance. She's twenty years old, and for nearly a year now she's been Kirby's mistress, while buzzing round Mrs. Kirby and making up to her . . .

"And would you believe it?—For a long time now it's been settled between her and her lover that he's to get a divorce and marry her . . .

"Only that needed money. To marry the daughter of Reichberg, the rich paper manufacturer. A lot of money, in fact.

"What more do you want? Like to know something of Bob? Plain Barman Bob in a white jacket and a napkin over his arm . . . Yes, and with a fine house at Versailles, and a grand car, and an income of four or five hundred thousand francs a year . . . All in tips. Not so bad, is it?"

Radek was getting worked up. That little harsh note of exasperation had crept into his voice again.

"All this time Joseph Heurtin would be earning about six hundred francs a month, pushing a delivery trike through the streets of Paris for ten or twelve hours a day."

"And how much would you?"

It was snapped out brutally while Maigret once more looked hard into the Czech's eyes.

"Oh! Me? . . ."

Neither spoke for a while. Maigret was now striding up and down the room, his hands in his trouser pockets, except for a moment when he stopped to put some more coal into the stove. Radek lit another cigarette.

It was a queer situation. For there was no clue that could enable Maigret to guess why his visitor was there at all. Certainly he seemed in no hurry to go. On the contrary, he looked as though he was waiting for something.

Maigret didn't want to ask him questions. That would only be playing into Radek's hand. Besides, what should he ask?

It was Radek who broke the silence:

"A beautiful crime . . . I'm speaking of Desmond Taylor's murder. He was alone in his room at a hotel. A young film star came to see him. She's seen to leave, but he does not show her out. He is later found dead in the room . . . You understand? . . . Yet it was not that girl that killed him . . ."

He was sitting in the chair that Maigret kept for visitors. So the light fell full on his face. It was a crude light, almost surgical. And the Czech's face had never been so interesting.

The forehead was high and bony. It was lined too, yet the lines hardly made the face look older. The long hair and the rather dark blue shirt with wide-open collar struck instantly the note of cosmopolitan bohemianism.

He wasn't thin, yet there was definitely something frail about him. His flesh didn't look firm. In the molding of the lips too there was a suggestion of ill health.

His excitement was expressed in a peculiar way that would have been interesting to a psychologist. Not a single feature moved—it was only the pupils of the eyes that seemed suddenly to be stepped up in voltage, giving his gaze an intensity that made others uncomfortable.

"What's to become of Heurtin?" he began again after a full five minutes' silence.

"The guillotine," sighed Maigret.

A little giggle from Radek. The voltage was now at its maximum.

"Naturally! . . . A man who earns six hundred francs a month. But to change the subject, let's make a bet. I bet you at William Kirby's funeral those two women will be in the deepest mourning and will weep on each other's shoulders— I mean Mrs. Kirby and Edna . . . But look here, inspector, I suppose you're quite sure he did really shoot himself?"

He laughed. It was quite unexpected. But then, with him everything was unexpected, most of all this visit.

"After all, it's so easy to dish up a murder as a suicide. It's very difficult to be sure. So much so that if I hadn't been at the time in the company of that charming young man, our good friend Janvier, I'd confess to murdering him myself, just to see what you'd do about it . . . Are you married?"

"What of it?"

"Nothing . . . But you're a lucky man . . . A wife. A modest situation. The satisfaction of doing your duty. On Sundays you go fishing—unless you happen to be a billiard player . . . Don't imagine I'm sneering. I think it's admirable . . . Only you've got to be born to that sort of thing. You've got to have a high-minded father who played billiards too."

"Where did you meet Joseph Heurtin?" said Maigret suddenly, trying to catch Radek off his guard. But he hadn't got the last word out before he regretted it.

"Where did I meet him? . . . In the newspapers. Just like everybody else . . . Unless, of course . . . Oh, dear! How complicated life is! . . . When I think of you there, listening to me, watching me, out of your depth, not knowing what to make of me . . . and when I think of all that's at stake: your career, your fishing, or your billiards . . . And at your age . . . Twenty years' service, perhaps more. Spotless record . . . And then to have the misfortune, for once in your life, to get an idea into your head and try and see it through . . . A sudden flash of genius . . . Genius, you know, is like everything else. You've got to start young. It's no use starting at forty-five. I suppose you're about that, aren't you?

"No, no. You ought to have left Heurtin to his fate. You might have been promoted . . . As a matter of fact, what's the pay of an inspector in the Police Judiciaire? Two thousand francs a month? Three perhaps? Say about half what Kirby used to spend in drinks. And when I say half—more likely a quarter. But let that go. How do you explain the suicide of that charming young man? A love affair? There'll be some nasty-minded people, naturally, who'll want to connect it with Joseph Heurtin's escape. And all the Kirbys and Hendersons, all those uncles, first cousins and second cousins who are something or other in America, will be sending cables asking for discretion . . .

"Really, if I were in your place . . ."

He got up, threw down his cigarette and stamped on it.

"In your place, inspector, I should try to create a diversion. I should, for instance, arrest some fellow that no banker or diplomat would dream of making a fuss about . . . Someone, let's say, like Radek, whose mother was a servant in Brno . . . How many people are there in Paris who even know where Brno is? . . ."

In spite of his self-possession there was a queer ring in his voice. And his foreign accent was stronger than Maigret had ever heard it before.

"But, you know, it's going to finish up much like the Taylor case . . . Only of course there are differences. In the Taylor case there were no fingerprints, no tracks of any kind . . . While here . . . Heurtin's fingerprints, Heurtin's footprints, Heurtin at Saint-Cloud in the Pavillon Bleu . . . Then Kirby, who so desperately needed money and who shoots himself when the investigations start again . . . And then me . . . But what have I got to do with it? . . .

"Kirby and I have never so much as spoken to each other. He didn't know me by name, and I don't think he even knew me by sight . . . And you might ask Heurtin if he's ever heard of a man called Radek . . . Then ask them at Saint-Cloud if they've ever seen anybody answering to my description . . . Yet here I am at the headquarters of the Police Judiciaire . . . I haven't been brought here, it's true. But I don't mind betting there'll be someone waiting downstairs to follow me about . . . And, by the way, I hope it'll always be Janvier . . . I should be most grateful . . . He's young, and such a nice fellow. Drink goes to his head at once—which, after all, is what it's meant for. Three cocktails, and he's floating in a sort of nirvana . . .

"Tell me, inspector, how can I send some money to a police charity? . . . I'd like to give a few thousand francs . . ."

In an offhand way he drew a bundle of notes from one of his pockets, put it back, and then took a similar bundle from another pocket. Then he opened his jacket and started on his waistcoat pockets. By the time he had finished he had produced the best part of a hundred thousand francs.

"Is that all you have to say to me?"

It was Radek speaking to Maigret with an annoyance he could not conceal.

"That's all."

"Well, shall I tell you one thing more?"

No answer.

"It's just this: you'll never understand the first thing about it."

He picked up his newly acquired black felt hat, and moved awkwardly to the door, obviously rather put out, while Maigret muttered to himself:

"Sing, my pretty bird! Sing!"

# MAIGRET BECOMES
# TALKATIVE

"How much do you earn in a day selling papers?"

They were sitting outside one of the cafés in Montparnasse. Radek, leaning back in his chair and smoking a Havana, was smiling more diabolically than ever.

A miserable old woman was threading her way between the tables, offering her evening papers in an unintelligible murmur to the people sitting there. She was absurd and pitiful from head to foot.

"How much do I . . . ?"

She hadn't taken it in, and from her vacant look one could tell at once that she possessed only the faintest flicker of intelligence.

"Sit down . . . We'll have a drink together . . . Waiter! A chartreuse for madame."

Out of the corner of his eye Radek shot a glance at Maigret, who was at another table only a few yards off.

"Look here! To start off, I'll buy all your papers . . . But you've got to count them."

Quite bewildered, the old creature did not know whether

to obey or to run away. But the Czech produced a hundred-franc note, and she began to count them feverishly.

"Here, drink this up . . . Forty, you say? . . . At twenty-five centimes apiece . . . But wait a moment, that's only ten francs. Would you like to earn a hundred?"

Maigret missed nothing of what was going on. Though from his face you would never have thought it.

"A hundred francs . . . Two hundred . . . three hundred . . . Here we are . . . Or let's make it five. Only, to earn it you'll have to sing us a song . . . Now! Keep your hands off. You've got to sing first."

"What shall I sing?"

She stood there gaping, quite unable to grasp the situation. A sticky drop of liqueur slowly ran down between the gray hairs on her chin. The people around began nudging one another.

"Sing anything you like . . . Something jolly . . . And if you dance you'll get a hundred francs extra . . ."

It was simply horrible. The wretch could not take her eyes off the money. In a faint voice she began to croak out some tune that was no tune at all, while all the time her hand was stretched out toward the money.

"That'll do," called out some people at the next table.

"Go on. Sing," ordered Radek, who kept on glancing at Maigret.

Protests arose on all sides now. A waiter came up and wanted to turn her away, but she stood her ground, clinging desperately to the hope of winning that fabulous sum.

"I'm singing for this young gentleman. He's promised me . . ."

The end was still more disgusting. A policeman came up and led her off without her having earned a single centime. A boy was sent after her to give her back her papers.

There were other scenes like that, ten at least, during the last five days before the end, during which Inspector Maigret, grim, sulky, obdurate, followed Radek, in and out, up and down, morning, noon, and night.

At first the Czech had attempted to renew their conversation. More than once he had suggested:

"Since you've made up your mind to dog my footsteps, let's keep each other company. It'll be so much more amusing."

But Maigret had not responded. At the Coupole and other cafés he would sit at a table where he could keep an eye on Radek. In the street he walked directly behind him.

Radek's nerves were on the stretch. Indeed, it had resolved itself into a battle of nerves.

William Kirby's funeral duly took place, mixing two different worlds, bankers and diplomats jostling the somewhat tawdry crowd from Montparnasse. And the two women duly fulfilled Radek's predictions. The latter was there too, calmly aloof, speaking to nobody.

Five days of it. A situation so unreal that it seemed more like a nightmare.

Now and again Radek would turn round to Maigret and try to talk:

"You still understand nothing."

But Maigret would pretend not to hear. His face was as blank as a wall. It was not more than once or twice in all those five days that Radek even managed to catch his eye.

He simply followed, that was all. He didn't seem to be watching for anything or waiting for anything. Just following, obstinately. Always there, minute after minute, hour after hour.

In the morning it would be a round of the cafés. Radek had apparently nothing else to do. Suddenly he would say to a waiter:

"I want to see the manager."

And when the manager came:

"Do your waiters generally serve their customers with dirty hands?"

He usually paid with a hundred-franc or a thousand-franc note, shoveling the change carelessly into whichever pocket was most handy. At restaurants he found fault with the food and often sent it away. One day, after a lunch that cost him 150 francs, he said to the head waiter:

"There'll be no tips. The service was not good enough."

At night they went around from café to cabaret, from cabaret to café. In the cabarets he would stand drinks to the girls, and flaunt his money before them till they were all agog with excitement. And once he then suddenly threw a thousand-franc note into the middle of the room, saying:

"Here! Scramble for it."

Of course there was a free fight. One woman was chucked out of the place. And as usual Radek looked at Maigret to see if he showed any signs of being impressed.

Only once did he try to shake his follower off. And Maigret, certain to find him before long back in the Coupole, had no hesitation in letting him succeed. On the evening before the funeral Radek disappeared for a good three hours. Apart from this occasion, he never once gave Maigret any trouble. On the contrary, whenever he took a taxi, he would wait till the inspector had found one too.

William Kirby's funeral took place on October 22. On the 23rd Radek dined in a restaurant not far from the Champs-Élysées. He had got there late and was still lingering over his coffee at eleven o'clock.

At half past he left, followed by Maigret. He took care to choose a comfortable taxi and gave the address in a low voice. A minute or two later two taxis, one behind the other, were making in the direction of Auteuil.

You would have looked in vain for any trace of emotion on the detective's broad face. Nor would you have seen either impatience or fatigue. Yet he hadn't been to bed for days. The only thing you might have noticed was that the eyes had a slightly fixed stare.

Radek's taxi followed the right bank of the Seine, crossed the river by the Pont Mirabeau, and slowed down over the bumpy road leading to the Citanguette.

When still a hundred yards away, he stopped the cab, said something to the driver, and with his hands in his pockets walked down to the quay right in front of the inn. He sat down on a bollard, looked around to make sure Maigret had followed, then lit a cigarette and waited.

Minutes passed. Midnight came and went. Nothing had happened. Three Arabs were throwing dice in the bar, while a man who had had a glass too many was sleeping in a corner. The proprietor was washing up. There was no light in any of the windows upstairs.

At five past twelve another taxi came bumping along over the ruts and drew up in front of the Citanguette. A woman got out and, after a moment's hesitation, went inside.

Radek looked at Maigret in the darkness. His eyes in daylight would have appeared more sarcastic than ever. The woman was now right under the unshaded light in the bar. She had on a black coat with a high fur collar, which hid half her face. Even so, it was impossible not to recognize Mrs. Kirby.

She leaned over the bar and spoke in a low voice to the proprietor. The Arabs stopped playing and stared.

What she said was inaudible, but from outside they could sense the woman's embarrassment and the man's surprise.

A moment or two later he turned toward the stairs behind the bar and went up. She followed. Then a room above was lit up, the room Joseph Heurtin had slept in after his escape.

The man came down alone. The Arabs started asking questions. As he answered, he gave a shrug to his shoulders that seemed to say:

"I'm just as much in the dark as you are. But what business is it of ours?"

The room upstairs had no shutters and the curtains were cheap and flimsy. Through them the two watchers outside could follow most of her movements.

"A cigarette, inspector?"

Maigret, barely five paces from Radek, did not answer. Mrs. Kirby looked as though she was stripping the bed.

She was lifting something heavy. Then she was bending over, intent on some strange occupation. At one moment she stopped and made a move toward the window, as though suddenly anxious, but she returned at once to what she was doing.

"It almost looks as though she had a grudge against that mattress. If you ask me, she's ripping it open . . . A queer job for her to undertake. Why didn't she bring her maid?"

A quarter of an hour went by.

"Dear me! It's getting more and more complicated."

Radek's voice betrayed his eagerness, but Maigret neither moved nor spoke.

It was just after half past twelve when Mrs. Kirby reappeared in the bar downstairs. She threw some money onto the zinc counter and, putting up her coat collar, ran back to the taxi that was waiting for her.

"Shall we follow her, inspector?"

It was now a procession. Three taxis, following each other across the river. On the other side they turned, not toward Paris, but in the direction of Saint-Cloud.

Mrs. Kirby did not drive right up to the Hendersons'

house, but stopped her taxi a little way off. She looked very small as she walked along the pavement on the other side of the road, hesitating from time to time.

Suddenly she crossed the road, went quickly through the garden gate, took a key from her handbag, and opened the front door, shutting it gently behind her.

No lights were turned on. Only now and again there came a faint glow through the shutters on the first floor, as though someone had struck a match. It was a cold damp night. Around each street lamp was a faint misty halo.

Radek and Maigret had stopped their taxis farther off still, a good two hundred yards from the house. Maigret got out and paced up and down by his taxi, his hands in his pockets, puffing furiously at his pipe.

"Well?" asked Radek. "Aren't you going to see what she does?"

But Maigret merely went on walking up and down.

"You may be making a mistake, inspector. Just imagine . . . Suppose they find another corpse in the house to-morrow?"

Still Maigret made no response. Radek fingered the cigarette he was smoking, tore it to shreds, threw it on the ground.

"I've told you a hundred times you'd never understand. I tell you again, you . . ."

But Maigret turned his back.

Nearly an hour went by. Everything was quiet. No light at all in the house now, not even that faint intermittent glow.

Mrs. Kirby's driver was getting anxious. He had got

down from his seat and gone up to the gate through which she had disappeared.

"Suppose there was someone else in the house, inspector . . . ?"

Maigret turned and stared at him so hard that he broke off and said no more.

When Mrs. Kirby left the house, a few moments later, she was carrying something about a foot long wrapped in white paper, or perhaps a cloth. She ran to her taxi and drove off.

"Aren't you curious to know what . . . ?"

"Look here, Radek!"

"What?"

Mrs. Kirby's taxi was nearly out of sight, yet Maigret showed no sign of following. The Czech was getting more and more agitated. His lips trembled slightly.

"Shall we go and take a look round?"

"But . . ."

Radek hesitated. He was like a man who has made the most perfect arrangements and then suddenly begins to wonder whether they are not going wrong.

Maigret patted him heavily on the shoulder.

"If we put our heads together we ought to be able to understand everything. Don't you think so?"

Radek laughed, but it was not convincing.

"Well? Would you rather not come?" went on Maigret. "Perhaps you're afraid of finding a corpse. Didn't you say something about a corpse just now? . . . Nonsense. Whose could it be? Mrs. Henderson's dead and buried. Élise Cha-

trier's dead and buried. William Kirby's dead and buried.
His wife's just gone off in a taxi, so she's alive enough . . .
And Joseph Heurtin is safely stowed away in the sick
quarters of the Santé . . . Who's left? Edna perhaps? But
what would she be doing here?"

"I'll come with you," growled Radek.

"Good. Then let's begin at the beginning. To get into a
house one needs a key.

"Here we are. So now we can walk right in and make
ourselves at home. Since there's nobody in the house—we
agree about that, don't we? . . ."

It was no longer the same situation. Somehow the tables had been turned. The triumphant look of sarcasm had
given way to a look of confused anxiety that Radek could
not suppress.

They were in the house now. Maigret switched on the
lights in the hall. He knocked out his pipe against the heel
of his boot and refilled it.

"Let's go up . . . You see, the man who killed Mrs. Henderson had a pretty easy job . . . Two sleeping women. No
concierge. No dogs . . . Nothing to worry about . . ."

Maigret did not even bother to look at his companion.

"But you know, Radek, you were quite right about the
corpse. Yes, that would be a nasty surprise . . . Have you
ever heard of Monsieur Coméliau, the examining magistrate? A man who can make himself very nasty when he
wants to. And he's got a down on me already for having let
Kirby shoot himself. You see, I was more or less there at
the time. In fact, he's fed up with the whole business.

"Another corpse, indeed! There *would* be a hullabaloo. And I should be properly in the soup for having let Mrs. Kirby sail off like that without even finding out what she was carrying. As for you, how could you be implicated? You haven't been out of my sight the whole evening.

"In fact, for the last week we've been seeing a good deal of each other, haven't we? By the way, there's one thing I'd like to know: Am I following you, or are you following me? . . ."

He rambled on, apparently quite indifferent as to whether the other was listening. They were on the first floor now, and, having crossed the boudoir, were entering the bedroom where Mrs. Henderson had been killed.

"Come in, Radek, come in. You're not squeamish, are you? I don't suppose it makes any odds to you that a couple of women were knifed to death in the place. By the way, we never found that knife. Heurtin was presumed to have thrown it in the river as he went away."

Maigret was sitting on the edge of the bed, just where the old woman's body had been found.

"And yet, you know, I'm not so sure that it was. In fact, I've come to the conclusion that it might, after all, have been hidden here . . . What was it Mrs. Kirby was carrying just now? . . . Do you see what I'm getting at? Something about a foot long. Wouldn't that be just about the size of a good dagger? . . . You're quite right, Radek. You're quite right . . . This case is getting more and more complicated all the time . . . Hallo! What's this?"

He was leaning over the polished parquet floor, where

footprints were clearly visible in the dust that had settled. Heel marks, particularly. The heel marks of a woman's shoes.

"Have you got good eyesight? If you have, you might help me follow these. We might even find out just what Mrs. Kirby came for."

Radek wavered, like a man who's not sure whether or not he's being made a fool of. But he could read nothing in the detective's face.

"They seem to be leading into the other bedroom. Look! Here they go. Come on, old chap, you're not helping at all. Get down to it. You haven't got fourteen stone to bend . . . Here's another . . . Then there . . . Hallo! They're going to that cupboard. Is there a lock to it? . . . No. But we mustn't be in too much of a hurry to open it. We mustn't forget that corpse of yours. Suppose it's there . . . ?"

Radek lit a cigarette. His hands were trembling.

"All the same, we've got to face it . . . Just open the door, will you?"

As he spoke, Maigret put his tie straight in the mirror, though he did not lose sight of Radek.

"Well? Go on."

Radek opened the cupboard door.

"Hallo! What's this? That doesn't look like a corpse to me."

Radek had stepped back. He was staring in amazement at a fair-haired girl who stepped out of the cupboard awkwardly, but showing no sign of fear.

It was Edna Reichberg. She looked from one to the

other of the two men as though expecting an explanation. She did not seem worried, showing merely the embarrassment of someone who has been asked to play a part.

Maigret, however, took no notice of her inquiring look, but turned to Radek, who was struggling to regain his self-possession.

"Now what do you say to that? We thought we'd find a corpse—at least that's what you'd been leading me to expect—and out steps a charming young lady as alive as could be."

Edna too was now looking with curiosity at the Czech.

"Well, Radek, what are we to make of it?" Maigret went on genially.

Silence.

"Do you still think I'm floundering in the dark? What?"

The girl, who was still staring at Radek, opened her mouth to scream, but fright had paralyzed her voice. No sound came.

Maigret had turned back to the mirror. He had removed his hat and was smoothing down his hair with the palm of his hand.

And Radek had whipped out a revolver, aimed it at the inspector, and pulled the trigger.

So Edna tried to scream, but couldn't. Yet really it was more comic than frightening. Just a little metallic click, hardly louder than what a toy pistol would have made. No bang, no bullet.

And again Radek pressed the trigger. Again the silly little click.

The end was so swift that it was all over in a moment. Edna saw the detective standing there so solidly before her . . . And in half a second Radek was writhing on the floor with Maigret on top of him. Fourteen stone—that's what he'd said. Quite enough to knock the breath out of your body.

Radek was in handcuffs.

"Forgive me, mademoiselle," said Maigret, getting to his feet. "It's all over now. There's a taxi waiting for you down the road. Radek and I will take the other one. We've got such a lot to tell each other . . ."

Radek had risen to his feet. He was wild with fury. But Maigret's heavy hand came down once more with a good-natured slap on the young man's shoulder.

"We have, sonny, haven't we?"

# 11

# FOUR ACES

From three o'clock onward the light was burning in Maigret's room at the Préfecture. The few people who went along the corridor during the early hours of the morning could hear a monotonous murmur through the door.

At eight o'clock the inspector sent out for two *petits déjeuners*. Then he telephoned to Monsieur Coméliau at his house.

It was nine o'clock before the door opened and Radek appeared, followed by Maigret. Radek was no longer in handcuffs.

Both men looked utterly exhausted. On the other hand, on neither of their faces was there the faintest trace of animosity.

"Is this the way?" asked Radek when they got to the end of the passage.

"Yes. We'll cut across the Palais de Justice. It's shorter that way."

And Maigret took him to the Dépôt by the private passage reserved for the Préfecture de Police. The formalities were soon through. As a warder marched Radek off to a cell, Maigret looked at the young man he had been studying so

closely. It seemed as though he wanted to say something—
just some little parting word—but he could not find it, and
with an almost imperceptible shrug of the shoulders he
walked slowly off to Monsieur Coméliau's office.

———

The examining magistrate was trying not to look like a
man in the wrong. As soon as he heard the knock on the
door, he opened a file and turned over some papers as casually as he could.

But he could have saved himself the trouble, for Maigret had not come to crow. There was not the least sign of
triumph or sarcasm on the detective's face. He simply
showed the drawn features of a man who has finished a
long and painful task.

"You don't mind my smoking? . . . Thanks . . . It's cold
in here."

And he threw a venomous glance at the radiator. He
loathed central heating, and had insisted on its being done
away with in his own room, to be replaced by a proper old-
fashioned stove.

"It's all over now . . . As I told you over the telephone,
he has confessed. And I don't think he's going to give you
any trouble. He's a good loser."

Maigret looked down at the notes he had written on
odd scraps of paper. They were to help him write up his report. But they were all in a jumble, and he pushed them
back into his pocket with a sigh.

"The outstanding feature of this case . . ." he began, but that was altogether too pompous a phrase for him.

He got up and began pacing up and down, his hands behind his back.

"The whole thing was faked right from the start. And it was the murderer himself who told me so. And there has been more faking about it than even he imagined.

"When Joseph Heurtin was arrested, what struck me most of all was the impossibility of fitting his crime into any sort of pigeonhole. He didn't know the victims; he made no attempt to steal anything; he was neither a sadist nor a madman.

"When I started afresh on the investigations I became more and more convinced that we had been following false tracks all the time. And not merely false—faked, deliberately and scientifically faked. Faked with a skill that completely diddled the police and led the Seine Assizes into giving a wrong verdict.

"And the murderer—this is the interesting point—was the biggest fake of all.

"You and I both know something of criminal types. Well, I can assure you, neither of us knew anything about the type called Radek.

"For a week now I've been living with him, watching him, trying to get inside his thoughts. And for a week I've been driven from wonder to amazement, and then from amazement to stupor.

"A mentality that defies classification. And he would

never have been in the smallest danger if he hadn't been guided by some obscure instinct to give himself away. That's why I call him a fake.

"For it was he himself who put me on the right track. He knew he was doing it. Yet he couldn't help doing it . . .

"And now that his number's up, he's more relieved than anything else . . ."

Maigret did not raise his voice. But he spoke with a quiet, contained vehemence that gave his words a peculiar force. They could hear people going to and fro in the corridor of the Palais de Justice, sometimes the heavy tread of policemen, but more often the lighter steps of clerks. Now and again a name was called out.

"A man who murdered for no real motive at all. Just for murder's sake. But no, it's not quite so simple as that either. I might almost say to amuse himself . . . O yes! you'll see . . .

"In a way, there was motive enough—money. But then he didn't bother to collect it . . . Yes, you'll see. Though I don't think you'll get much out of him. For there's only one thing he wants now—to be left in peace. He told me so himself.

"His mother was a servant in Brno. He was brought up in some kind of institution little better than a prison. But he got scholarships and was helped by various charities and in the end became a medical student.

"As a child he suffered, and at an early age began to hate the world which he could only look up at from below. At an early age, too, he became convinced he was a genius . . . To acquire fame and riches by the force of his intellect! . . . A dream which brought him across Europe, finishing up in Paris. A dream which enabled him to accept money from his mother, who, at the age of sixty-five and riddled by a disease of the spine, still worked as a servant so that he could finish his studies.

"A devouring pride. A pride goaded on by a feverish impatience, for he knew that he was afflicted by his mother's disease, in fact a more rapid form of it. He knew he hadn't many years to live.

"He worked like a slave. His professors regarded him as their most promising pupil. He had no friends. He never spoke much, even to his fellow students.

"He was poor, but he was used to poverty. Often he went to his classes with no socks under his shoes. More than once he worked in the market unloading vegetables to earn a few coppers . . .

"Then came the catastrophe. His mother died. There was no more money.

"And suddenly, without any transition, he turned his back on all his dreams. He might have looked for work, as so many students do. But no, he didn't lift a finger . . .

"Had he got a suspicion that he wasn't quite the genius he'd imagined? Had he begun to lose confidence in himself? In any case, he did nothing. Nothing whatever. He merely loafed about in the cafés, writing begging letters to distant relations and appealing to charitable organizations: He sponged cynically on any Czechs he happened to meet in Paris, even flaunting his lack of gratitude.

"The world hadn't understood him. So he hated the world. And he spent his time nursing his hatred. In the Montparnasse cafés he would sit among people who were rich, happy, and bursting with good health. He would sip his *café-crème* while cocktails were being poured out by the gallon.

"Is he already toying with the idea of a crime? Perhaps . . . I really don't know. But I know that twenty or thirty years ago he'd have been a militant anarchist chucking bombs at royalty. But that's no longer fashionable these days . . .

"He's alone, isolated, stewing in his isolation. Prides himself on it, revels in it, and feels more and more superior.

"His intelligence is certainly remarkable. Still more remarkable his flair for sensing the weaknesses of others. One of his professors talked to me about him. It seems that at the school of medicine he was positively feared on account of this gift. He had only to look at a man for a few minutes to spot the defects of his constitution.

"Meeting a man for the first time, he would say to him with malicious delight:

"'Within three years you'll be in a sanatorium.'

"Or:

"'Your father died of cancer, didn't he? Take care!'

"His gift for diagnosis was simply astonishing. And not only medically—morally too. In the Coupole it was his only occupation. Just to sit there and *diagnose* . . . All sorts of taints and weaknesses, physical and moral.

"Kirby of course came within range of his guns, and he gave me a most vivid picture of the man. Looking at Kirby, I must admit, I'd seen no more than a spoiled boy myself, a nice-mannered, frivolous man about town. Radek had seen another side altogether.

"He sketched for me a happy-go-lucky Kirby, beloved by women, by everybody, and enjoying all the good things of life—but also a Kirby ready to put his hand to any dirty meanness to satisfy his thirst for pleasure . . .

"A Kirby who could let his wife live on terms of closest friendship with his mistress, Edna Reichberg. While all the time he was conspiring with Edna to get a divorce and marry her.

"A Kirby who was not above forging his relations' signatures, and who finally in a careless moment dropped the mask altogether . . .

"It was one evening when he was sitting in the bar of the Coupole with two of his innumerable friends. His wife and Edna had just gone off to the theater. Putting down the evening paper with a snort, he said:

"*To think that this fool could kill an old woman for a matter of twenty-two francs—that's all she had in the till—while I'd give a hundred thousand to anyone who'd get rid of my aunt for me!*'

"What was it? Just a flippant remark? An idle boast? . . . But Radek was there . . .

"Radek hated Kirby more than all the others, because he was the most sparkling specimen of the social whirl he so much resented. And he knew Kirby better than Kirby knew himself. On the other hand, Kirby had never stopped to look at Radek . . .

"Radek got up and went to the lavatory. On a bit of paper he scribbled:

"'*Ready to earn the 100,000 francs. Send key, initials M. V., poste restante, Boulevard Raspail.*'

"When he got back to his seat, a waiter from another part of the café had just handed Kirby the note. The latter read it with a laugh, and then went on with the conversation. But his eyes kept wandering, scrutinizing the other people in the bar.

"A quarter of an hour later he called for some poker dice.

"'Playing all by yourself?' asked one of his friends.

"'Just an idea . . . I want to see if I can throw at least two aces the first go . . .'

"'And if you do?'

"'Then it'll be *yes.*'

"'Yes to what?'

"'Nothing important . . . Just an idea . . .'

"He shook the dice for a long time, and Radek could see his hand was trembling.

"'Four aces!'

"Kirby wiped his forehead and got up to go. He made some jocular remark to one of the others, but it sounded hollow.

"And Radek got the key."

Maigret was now sitting astride of a chair, leaning over the back. It was his favorite position.

"It was Radek who told me this story of the dice. I'm sure it's true. I've sent Janvier round to the Coupole to see if he can find out anything that would corroborate it, though it's rather late in the day for that.

"As for the rest, for the last few days I've had a pretty shrewd idea what happened. Radek's story this morning has only filled in the gaps. Though of course it's all thanks to him . . . Little by little he gave me the hints I needed.

"Just think of Radek in possession of that key! He could now get even with the world . . . It wasn't the money. I don't think that hundred thousand francs really interested him at all. He wanted much more than that . . . And he'd got it . . .

"He'd got Kirby—Kirby, the bright young spark, the envy of Montparnasse—right in the hollow of his hand. That key meant power . . .

"At the best he hadn't many years to live, perhaps only a few. He had no attachments of any kind . . . Can you wonder if . . . ?

"I said just now that if he'd been born a generation earlier he'd have been an anarchist. But in our day, and belonging to that jumpy, unstable, bohemian crowd, it wasn't in his line at all . . . Something much more interesting, much more exciting—*a really grand crime!*

"A grand crime . . . He's a pauper and a sick man, yet the papers will be full of one of his actions. He had only to lift a finger, and the whole machinery of police and justice will start turning. An old woman will lie dead and a Kirby will tremble . . .

"And he'd be the only one to know, sitting there at the Coupole over his *café-crème*, a student nobody takes any notice of . . . But powerful . . .

"Of course he mustn't get caught. And to make sure of that, the best way was to get somebody else caught. He comes across Heurtin at a café. More diagnosis. And having sized him up, he gets talking to him.

"Heurtin is hardly better treated by the world than Radek. He might have led a peaceful life at home with his parents, but in his way he is ambitious. He's a day-dreamer, devours cheap novels, goes to the films, and pictures himself playing the hero in all sorts of marvelous adventures . . . But instead of that he's carrying around bunches of flowers for six hundred francs a month . . . A spineless fellow. No will. What defense could he put up against Radek?

"'Would you like to earn in a single night enough to live on for the rest of your life?'

"Heurtin's dreams are rosier than ever. Another creature in the hollow of Radek's hand. And Radek talks—so persuasively—and brings him around to the idea of a burglary . . .

"Just a burglary. And in an empty house.

"He works out a plan, down to the minutest details. Insists on Heurtin buying shoes with rubber soles. Even in an empty house it would be better not to make a noise! But of course it was really for the sake of the footprints.

"It must have been absolutely intoxicating for Radek. He hadn't enough money to buy himself a cocktail at the Coupole, yet he could juggle with human lives.

"Time passed. He was in no hurry. Almost daily he rubbed shoulders with this Kirby who did not know him from Adam. It must have been a grueling time for Kirby, waiting, knowing nothing; but he laughed and talked the same as ever . . .

"What finally opened my eyes to what had happened in the Hendersons' house was a sentence in the pathologists' report. It's a lesson to me. One can't read the experts' reports too carefully. It was only four days ago that this detail got through my skull:

"*'Several minutes after her death, Mrs. Henderson's body, which must have been on the edge of the bed, rolled to the ground.'*

"You'll agree that there was no reason for the murderer to touch the body again. For Mrs. Henderson was wearing no jewelry—nothing, in fact, but her nightgown . . .

"But let's get back to the story . . . Radek persuades Heurtin to enter the house, with a duplicate key he has had made, at *exactly* half past two. He is then to go upstairs without any light at all and grope his way to where he'd find the money, that is to say, to the exact spot where Mrs. Henderson's body will be lying. Radek swears there will be nobody in the house.

"At a quarter past two Radek went in, killed the two women, and was clear of the place a full five minutes before Heurtin was due to arrive.

"Having left the house, he watched Heurtin go in. Heurtin did just what he'd been told. And suddenly groping in the dark, his hands touched a body which then rolled to the ground. He was panic-stricken, switched on the light, saw the bodies, went up to them to see if they were dead, paddled in blood, and left traces everywhere.

"Dashing out of the house, he ran into Radek, who was waiting for him. Quite a different Radek now from the persuasive one he had known hitherto. A sneering, pitiless Radek.

"The scene between those two men must have been something monstrous. But what could a simple Heurtin do against the other? He didn't even know his name or where he lived.

"Radek showed him his rubber gloves and the socks he'd put over his shoes. There'd be no trace of him in the house.

"'You'll be convicted, my boy. They won't believe your story. *Nobody* will believe you. You'll be executed.'

"They walked across the Seine to Boulogne, where a taxi was waiting. It was Radek who spoke to the driver while shoving Heurtin into the cab. The driver never saw Heurtin clearly at all. That's why we never knew how he returned from Saint-Cloud.

"During the drive Radek went on talking:

"'If you keep your mouth shut I'll save you. Do you understand? I'll get you out of prison. It may be after one month, it may be after three. But I'll get you out without fail.'

"Two days later Heurtin was arrested. He seemed almost in a stupor. He just repeated over and over again that he was innocent, but he'd say no more.

"As matter of fact, he had told the whole story—to his mother . . .

"*And his mother did not believe him.* Wasn't that the best possible proof that Radek was right? Who else would believe him if his mother wouldn't? Better keep his mouth shut and trust Radek to keep his promise.

"Months went by. Heurtin in his cell was haunted by the memory of those two bodies and his hands sticky with blood. He still hoped. It was only that day when he heard them coming for No. 9 early in the morning that he finally broke down. But even then he wouldn't speak.

"Then at last he got the note with the plan of escape. I think he only half believed in it, but he carried out the instructions all the same. When he got out, however, he didn't know what to do with himself. He wandered aimlessly about the streets, finally flinging himself down on a bed in the Citanguette. Poor devil, I suppose it was something at any rate to sleep elsewhere than in the Quartier de la Grande Surveillance.

"Anyhow, that sleep seemed to do him good. For when Dufour tried to get his paper he acted pretty promptly.

"Once more he wandered about. What good was freedom to him? He'd no more money. Nowhere to go. Nobody to turn to. His father had not answered his letters from prison and had forbidden his mother and sister either to write or go to see him.

"And all because of Radek. If only he could get hold of Radek! . . .

"What did he want with him? Did he want to kill him? He hadn't got anything to kill him with, but in the state of mind he was in I dare say he might have strangled him . . . Or did he simply want to find the only man he could now look in the face? . . .

"He began hunting, going around one after the other all the cafés where he'd been with him. For the two had always met at a café.

"At last he saw him in the bar at the Coupole. They wouldn't let him in, as by this time he was looking like a beggar. He waited outside, turning around and around, going backward and forward, now and again shoving his pasty face against the window . . .

"When Radek went out it was between two policemen. So that was no good, and once more Heurtin was an aimless wanderer.

"Then as a last hope, or perhaps instinctively, he turned toward Nandy, to the house that was now shut to him . . . But where else could he go?

"He slunk around to the back of the house and hid in a shed. But when his father found him and told him to clear out, he preferred to hang himself rather than start wandering again . . ."

—

Maigret shrugged his shoulders and sighed.

"He'll never make good . . . Oh, he'll live all right. But

he'll never get over it, never be anything else other than one of Radek's victims.

"There were victims enough already, and another one to come. And there might have been more still if . . . But we'll get to that later . . .

"So the crime was done, and Heurtin was in prison, and Radek as usual was camping most of the day in the American bar of the Coupole.

"Radek was still as poor as ever, for he didn't demand his hundred thousand francs. Why didn't he? At first he hesitated, fearing a trap. He wanted to see Heurtin convicted first, and the case closed down. But there was more than that in it. Much more. He'd come to enjoy his poverty. It fed his hatred of the world . . .

"Besides, poverty plus power—there was something picturesque about that, dramatic even. And then there was the exquisite pleasure of keeping Kirby dangling in suspense.

"Kirby was still frequenting the Coupole, outwardly as gay as ever. Only Radek knew that his laugh was hollow. Kirby was puzzled. Like the rest of the world, he thought Heurtin was guilty, and wondered whether the murderer would denounce him.

"But he didn't. At the Assizes Heurtin put up practically no defense at all and was duly convicted. How impatient Kirby must have been for the execution, after which he could breathe freely again.

"Is Radek satisfied? Not altogether. He has had his grand crime and the whole plan had worked out perfectly.

Not a breath of suspicion has come his way. He is the only one in the world to know the whole truth—that's just what he'd wanted. And he can look with infinite disdain at the Kirbys and their futile gang gossiping over their cocktails.

"And yet he isn't satisfied . . . Something's lacking.

"I couldn't swear to it, but I wouldn't mind betting that what was lacking was somebody to admire what he'd done, somebody who could say:

"'Do you see that man? He doesn't look anything special. But I can tell you he has committed one of the most perfect crimes of the century. He has beaten the police, tricked the Courts of Justice, and altered the course of half a dozen lives.'

"It has been that way with other murderers. Most of them have had to confide in somebody, if only a prostitute. Radek is stronger than that; and anyhow he has never been particularly interested in women . . .

"The papers say one morning that Heurtin has escaped. Isn't that just his opportunity? Things are moving again: he won't be left out. Wheels are turning: he'll put a spoke in them. After all, this is his crime and nobody else's! So he writes the letter to the *Sifflet*.

"He has neatly avoided Heurtin by getting himself arrested. Another triumph! And he's now thoroughly worked up. He wants admiration, does he? Well, what admiration could be sweeter than that of the police? So he comes to me and says:

"'You'll never understand the first thing about it.'

"From that moment onward it was a delirious, head-long downfall. He was bound to be caught in the end, but the game was too fascinating. He'd played with Heurtin and Kirby easily. But now he had come to the big stuff: he was going to play with me.

"He did all he could to intrigue me. He threw out suggestions to send me off on false trails. He drew my attention, for instance, to the fact that all the events of the case had taken place on the banks of the Seine.

"All the time he was making hints and allusions, some true, some false. He was living in a fever. Flirting with disaster. He must have known he was lost, but . . .

"But he was lost anyway. Don't forget that. A condemned man. Nothing to live for. All that other men respected either disgusted or angered him.

"Anyhow, if he was to fall, Kirby was to fall too. So he telephoned him to demand the hundred thousand francs. He showed them to me. What an actor! What a clown! Didn't I say he was a fake?

"It was he who made Kirby go to the house at Saint-Cloud. Another bit of psychological astuteness. He'd seen me just before, for I called in at the Coupole after getting back from Nandy. He knew I was reinvestigating the case. Wouldn't I naturally take it up from the beginning? In other words, wouldn't I go back to Saint-Cloud?

"I wasn't bound to go there that afternoon, but there was quite a good chance of it. And if I didn't, he could send Kirby back there as often as he liked. Kirby could refuse him nothing.

"And if I found Kirby there, Kirby might be very embarrassed. Something might happen . . .

"It may be just his vanity, but he certainly prides himself on Kirby's death. And on the whole I'm inclined to think . . . But still we'll never know . . .

"Another feather in his cap. His sense of power became more intoxicating than ever. And it was because I could see the fever in his eyes that I stuck to him day in, day out, obstinately silent and morose.

"How long would his nerves hold out? Many little things combined to tell me that he was on a dangerous slope . . . He needed constantly to indulge his hatred of the world. He humiliated the people who had to serve him, made a fool of an old woman selling papers, got a crowd of girls to fight for a thousand-franc note.

"And every time he watched to see what impression it would make on me.

"He was getting near the precipice. Sooner or later he'd lose his head and make a fatal slip.

"He did. The greatest criminals come to it in the end.

"He had killed two women. He had killed Kirby—or at least he thought so. He had made Heurtin a wreck for life. But still it was not enough. The curtain was still up, so the play must go on . . .

"But I'd taken a few precautions. Janvier was posted at the Hôtel George V with instructions to intercept all letters and telephone calls for either Mrs. Kirby or Edna Reichberg.

"One evening—it was three days ago—I realized that

Radek was anxious to shake me off. It was my policy to give him all the rope he wanted, so I let him go. If he tried to get away altogether there was mighty little chance of his succeeding. For one thing, I still had his passport in my possession.

"The following morning I was given two letters that he had posted.

"The first was for Mrs. Kirby, telling her that the murder had been committed at her husband's instigation. To prove it he sent her the key he had received and the box it had come in. The address on the box was in Kirby's writing.

"Radek further told her that in French law a murderer could not inherit money from his victim. Thus the whole of her fortune was liable to be seized.

"He ordered her to go at midnight to the Citanguette and to open up the mattress of a certain room and look in it for the knife with which her aunt had been killed. When she found it, she was to take it away and hide it.

"If it wasn't there, she was to go to the Hendersons' house and look in a cupboard.

"You see this craving to humiliate people and at the same time to weave complications. Of course she would find nothing in the mattress, but it was fun to send this rich American woman on an absurd errand to a low-down bar for factory hands and bargees.

"And that's not all. He then went on to say that Edna was her husband's mistress and that they had arranged to get married. He finished the letter by saying:

*"'She knows the truth. She hates you, and she's going to inform the police so as to reduce you to penury.'"*

---

Maigret mopped his brow and sighed once more.

"Seems idiotic, doesn't it? But there's more to it than that, as you'll see. Radek had spent the last two years inventing subtle forms of revenge. He wasn't only thinking of making a fool of Mrs. Kirby."

"But the knife?" asked Coméliau. "You don't mean to say . . ."

"That it's been there all the time? No. Radek had to go back to Saint-Cloud and put it in a cupboard. And that was what he was up to when he gave me the slip that evening. At the same time he posted the two letters.

"A second key—the one he'd had made for Heurtin—was sent to Edna Reichberg with a letter saying that it was Kirby himself who had committed the crime, but that she could save his good name by going at a specified time and removing the knife that was hidden in the cupboard. He added that Mrs. Kirby had all along been in the secret.

"I tell you it was megalomania. He felt like a demigod playing with human fates.

"Do you see now the situation he was preparing?

"Mrs. Kirby, deeply shocked by his letter and still further upset by the sordid little comedy she is made to play at the Citanguette, comes into the room where the murder has been committed. Imagine the state of her nerves . . . And then to find herself face to face with Edna with a dagger in her hand—Edna whom she now knows to be her enemy.

"Would there have been another crime? We can't tell. But certainly Radek had planned one. And Radek's plans are not to be despised.

"Well, I had those two letters that had never reached their destinations. Like the letter addressed to the *Sifflet*, they were written with the left hand. We should have had a hard job to prove he'd written them.

"So what I did was this: I asked the two women to help me, saying it was to find Mrs. Henderson's murderer. I asked them to do just what Radek told them to do in the letters . . .

"It was Radek himself who led me to the Citanguette and then to Saint-Cloud. I knew he would.

"Outside the Citanguette he enjoyed himself immensely, but at Saint-Cloud he was beside himself with impatience to know what was going on inside the house. He even suggested there might be another corpse to be discovered. And yet, when Mrs. Kirby left and I asked him to come in with me, he hesitated. Things seemed to be turning out wrong, for he had expected me to follow Mrs. Kirby.

"Still, he followed me up, and it was he who opened the cupboard, though not to find a corpse, for out stepped Edna as trim as ever.

"He looked at me. He understood . . . And then finally he did what I expected. He drew out his revolver and pulled the trigger."

Monsieur Coméliau stared blankly.

"It's all right. Nothing happened. As I told you just now, I'd taken a few precautions. I'd sent one of my men to look for a revolver in his room. When he found it he reloaded it with dummies.

"That's all . . . He gambled and lost."

Maigret's pipe had gone out and he lit it again. Then he got up and stood looking into the far corner of the room with a frown on his forehead.

"And I must say he knows how to lose. He was wild at first, but only for a moment. We've spent the rest of the night together. I told him frankly what I knew, and asked him for the rest. He stalled a bit at first, but soon came clean . . .

"Then he talked straightforwardly enough, except for a touch of boastfulness . . . And now it's all over, he's amazingly calm. He asked me whether he'd be executed, and when I hesitated he said with a laugh:

"'Arrange it for me if you can, inspector . . . I think you owe it me . . . You see, I've got an idea . . . I once witnessed an execution in Germany . . . And at the last moment the condemned man, who'd been steady as a rock, suddenly burst into tears and started whining: "Mother!"

"'And I'm interested to know whether I'll do the same. What do you think?'"

———

For a minute or more neither of them spoke. In the silence they were once more conscious of the footsteps in the corridors of the Palais and of the distant and confused murmur of Paris.

Finally Monsieur Coméliau pushed away the file he had opened at the beginning of the interview.

"Good, inspector. Good!" he began. "I . . ."

He looked away. The blood mounted to his cheeks.

"I would like you to forget the . . . the . . ."

But Maigret, who had been putting on his coat, now held his hand out in the most natural manner in the world.

"You'll get my report tomorrow. I must go now and see Moers. I've promised him these letters. He wants to make a thorough study of them."

After a moment's hesitation he went to the door, where he just cast a quick glance back at the penitent expression on the examining magistrate's face. When he finally left the room there was the suggestion of a smile on his face.

It was his only revenge.

## 12

# A PARTING SHOT

January had come. It was freezing hard. The ten men who were present had their coat collars turned up and their hands in their pockets.

They stamped their feet to keep warm, exchanged desultory remarks, and now and again threw furtive glances in the same direction.

One man, however, was standing all by himself, his neck disappearing into his shoulders, his face so disagreeable that no one dared to speak to him. It was Maigret.

The dawn was just beginning. Windows were lit up here and there in the neighboring blocks of flats. From time to time the gong of a tram rang out somewhere in the distance.

At last the sound of a van drawing up, the slam of a door, the tread of heavy boots, some orders given in an undertone.

A journalist was taking notes. He was ill at ease. Another man turned his back.

Radek, who had jumped briskly out of the prison van, was looking around him with his pale-blue eyes, which in the twilight had a remote and infinitely vague expression.

He was held by either arm, but that didn't seem to bother him as he walked with steady stride toward the scaffold.

The paving stones were icy. And suddenly Radek slipped and fell. The two warders, thinking he was trying to break away, pounced on him at once.

It was only a matter of a second or two, but this fall was perhaps more distressing than all the rest. What was so painful was Radek's shamefaced look as he got to his feet. He had quite lost the air of cool self-possession he had so carefully assumed.

His eyes fell on Maigret, whom he had particularly requested to be present, and who was now pretending he had not seen the young man's discomfiture.

"So you've come . . ." said Radek.

People were getting impatient. Nerves were on edge. Everybody wanted the business to be got through as quickly as possible.

But Radek looked back with a sneer at the place where he had fallen.

"That's spoiled it!"

The warders stood there hesitating, the men whose job it was to extinguish a human life.

Somebody spoke. A car horn hooted loudly in a nearby street.

It was Radek who stepped out first, looking straight in front of him.

"Inspector . . ."

In another minute, perhaps, it would be all over. The voice sounded strange.

"You'll be going home to your wife, won't you? . . . She'll have made the coffee by now."

The scene leaped to Maigret's mind, obliterating all else. It was the exact truth. His wife was waiting for him in their cozy little dining room, and the breakfast would be on the table . . .

And somehow, without knowing why, he could not face it. Instead, he went directly to the Quai des Orfèvres, where he started poking the fire so viciously that he nearly broke his precious stove.